HER DRAGON

BLACK CLAW DRAGONS: BOOK 6

Roxie Ray

© 2020

Disclaimer

This is a work of fiction. Names, places, characters and events are all fictitious for the reader's pleasure. Any similarities to real people, places, events, living or dead are all coincidental.

This book contains sexually explicit content that is intended for ADULTS ONLY (+18).

Contents

Chapter 1 - Kara

My phone buzzed with the sound of a calendar notification before my alarm went off. I felt blindly around my nightstand for my phone. My best friend and I had gone out for girls' time the night before, and I might've had a glass of wine too many. Waking up was the last thing I wanted to do.

Cracking an eye, I read the notification. Beneath the haze of a hangover, I was relieved to see I had plenty of time.

My new app had auto-booked me a job for the afternoon. I hadn't even had to take a phone call, which would have woken me up *and* forced me to be pleasant at the disgusting hour of ten in the morning. Not that most people considered ten to be that early, but it felt like it.

I loved technology.

I hadn't had any early jobs today, so I'd taken the rare chance to sleep in. I had drawn the curtains in my bedroom before collapsing on the bed, but it was still way too bright in here. Stumbling to my bathroom, I turned the light on long enough to grab the ibuprofen and choke two down with some tap water, then collapsed back on my bed and snatched my phone up again.

Clicking through the app, I pulled up the details for the job, then moaned. The gym again. Damn it. I hated doing jobs at the gym. The guys there were total dicks and just wanted to ogle me or talk about how they could do the job better. I couldn't even see them being able to handle their own tools, much less any of mine.

Ew. That thought came out wrong.

Whatever. I still had several hours before I had to be there, so I changed my alarm and went back to sleep.

The next time I woke, I felt much better. A shower and breakfast made all the difference toward making me feel like a human again. Not to mention the massive cup of coffee; that helped tremendously.

With a spring in my step, I drove to Main Street, then cut back a block to the gym. Turning off my truck, I sighed and looked up at the building. It used to be a warehouse, some plant that went under years ago. The current owner had converted it into a gym. Since it was the only gym in town, it was pretty popular.

But I didn't care how popular it was. There were a few die-hard members who were always there when I went to do whatever odd jobs the owner needed, and they delighted in being total dicks. The owner was never around to stop it, either.

Not that I wanted him to, I could handle my own shit. But still, he seemed like an okay guy and he had enough faith in my abilities to hire me, so he probably wouldn't have liked the guys harassing me. Maybe. Oh, well, at least the day was pretty. I tried hard to hang on to that positivity, but it was like trying to scoop water with a fork. It just wasn't happening.

Maybe I should've grabbed some coffee for the road, too.

With a big sigh, I grabbed my tool belt and stepped out of the truck. I had a tool bag, too, but wearing the belt made me feel more armored. My work clothes were simple: old jeans, a flannel shirt, and boots. It was good stuff for getting dirty in.

Even in such slouchy clothes, I felt like I was naked and on display walking into the gym. The belt was something of a security blanket and helped me feel even more covered.

I knew the problem the minute I stepped in, although my app had told me. The air was nearly suffocating, even with all the doors open, including the huge bay door in the back, and fans everywhere. We were right in the middle of the hottest part of summer, yet the gym bustled with activity. Men and women—mostly men—ran on treadmills, lifted weights, and a class that I was sure would normally be in a private room was dancing around out back, visible through the double doors.

A scrawny guy sat behind the counter playing on his cell phone. I couldn't help but wonder if he had the job so he could try to use the equipment for free to bulk up. Poor kid. "I'm here for the air conditioner," I said over the steady drone of the fans.

The kid pointed to a door without looking up. "Roof," he called. I nodded and walked quickly to the door before any other guys noticed I was there. A bead of sweat was already rolling down the back of my neck and I hadn't even gotten started yet. Gross.

"Hey, there."

Damn it. Some bulky guy had appeared out of freaking nowhere. I sighed and turned to face him, schooling my expression. I didn't want to be rude if it was just someone checking in. Or maybe someone that needed repairs done at home. If only I was ever that lucky. "Hello," I said politely. "How can I help?"

He smiled, and a dimple appeared in his overly tanned cheek. "I was just wondering what a pretty lady like you is doing in a job like this?"

My stomach turned over and my nose wrinkled in disgust. I pivoted on my boot heel and walked toward the door to the roof. He didn't deserve a reply.

"You'd be a lot cuter out of those men's clothes," he called. His chuckles followed me up the stairs, even after I was out of earshot. His words rang in my mind. Damn those guys. There wasn't any reason I couldn't do this job.

The air conditioning unit was an easy fix. I found the leak in a couple of minutes. I patched it with some duct tape just long enough to run to the hardware store and grab the hose I needed.

Since it was a beautiful day, I walked. It was pretty much a straight shot down the sidewalk anyway and finding parking this time of day was usually awful. All in all, I was back on the roof without further incident in a half hour and completed the job in about double that. Not bad for a day's work.

With a proud smile, I dusted my hands off and inspected my handiwork. Satisfied, I filled out the invoice and put all my tools back on my belt before heading back to the desk to drop off the paperwork with the kid at the counter.

Of course, two men were there, paying for smoothies. I had to admit, the fruity drinks did look good, but no way I was spending another minute in that gym. As quietly as I could, I waited behind the men and tried to sidestep them when they turned to walk away.

All I needed to do was slide the invoice across the counter and leave, but I recognized one of the men as soon as he turned around. Nick Summey. I'd gone to high school with him. He'd been the biggest dick in our class—or at least the second biggest, next to my ex. I had no reason to think he'd be any different today.

His gaze raked up and down my body like a creepy hug from an old pervert. "Kara?" he asked in an incredulous tone. "Is that you?"

"Yep." I stepped around him and slapped the invoice on the counter, then turned to leave without another word.

"Hang on, hang on, sweetheart." Nick reached out and grabbed my arm.

I froze, fury rushing through my body. I wasn't sure if I was angrier about the pet name or his hand on my arm.

Definitely his hand.

Slowly, I turned my head toward him but pointed my gaze to his hand on my arm without saying a word. It was a conscious effort not to use any number of my tools to remove it for him. Go, me.

Nick seemed to get the hint and let go of my arm. "Don't be hostile." His overly cheery voice held a dark undertone I didn't care for one bit. "I wanted to see if you'd like to get a drink with me sometime."

I turned my gaze to him as he elbowed his friend and laughed like a teenager in a locker room. "I mean, assuming you own clothes other than this. Or we could just skip to no clothes at all."

They both burst out laughing. The guy at the counter glanced up uncomfortably, then grabbed my invoice and turned away. Thanks for being a typical guy. I wouldn't know what to do with myself if men started calling each other out on their sexist behavior. I rolled my eyes.

"I think you can work the tomboy out of her," his friend said with a disgusting leer, his thick eyebrows waggling.

My fury turned white-hot. I no longer cared that I wanted to maintain a professional demeanor whenever possible. "Fuck you," I said in a low voice. "You immature pigs." They both sobered up and straightened. Their body language changed as I called them out, muscles tensing, eyebrows furrowing. "You're no better than idiotic high school boys. You're worse, actually, because at least they have the excuse of being young. You're grown-ass men, acting like a couple of complete fucking imbeciles."

"Listen here, you bitch," Nick said. "Nobody talks to me like that."

I chuckled and turned away. "I just did."

Someone stood right behind me. I hadn't heard him walk up, and I nearly ran him over when I turned to leave. Judging by his facial features, he was a Kingston. He looked too much like Maddox and Maverick. Like he could've been their brother, or a very close relative.

The expression on his face was like a thundercloud about to release a bolt of lightning.

Or fire. The light reflected in his hazel eyes as he turned his face from looking down at me and focused on the guys. For a split second, it looked like fire instead of a reflection. It would've been cool if I hadn't been so angry already.

"You need to watch your fucking mouth," the strange Kingston said in a gravelly voice. "And remember you're talking to a lady."

Shit, I wouldn't have gone that far. I wasn't exactly a lady, and I wasn't ashamed of that, but I appreciated the sentiment anyway.

Nick snorted. "She's no fucking lady."

He was technically right, but I also didn't need a guy, especially a random Kingston, coming in here to fight my battles. "Hey, I'm no damsel in distress. I can handle this," I said in a low voice while keeping my back to Nick and his friend and my eyes on Mr. Hottie Kingston. He was probably Mr. Annoying Kingston, too, but that was neither here nor there.

"Whatever," Nick said behind me. I still didn't give him the time of day. "She's not hot enough for me to bother, anyway." Their shoes scuffed on the concrete floor as they walked away. I tried to tune out their voices. I didn't need any more excuses to get pissed.

"Yes, she is," the stranger called.

Damn, it was hard not to giggle when he said that. It was cute. But still, I was too irritated. I cleared my throat.

"I'm sorry," he said as I tried to walk around him and finally make my escape. "You really didn't need my help. I just couldn't not say anything after what I heard that douchebag say to you."

I nodded but couldn't let him think women the world over needed men to fight their battles. "I appreciate the sentiment, but it was handled. Men like that don't need to think that the only reason they have to back off is because a woman has a different man in her corner."

His eyebrows crinkled, and he opened his mouth to argue, then cocked his head. "Is it like how sometimes when women are in a bar, and they tell a man they're not interested, and the man won't take no for an answer, but if the woman says she's in a relationship, they'll back off?"

"Sometimes even that doesn't work." I raised my eyebrows. "But I'm kind of surprised you know that's a problem."

He shrugged. "I read magazines sometimes."

Maybe I'd misjudged him.

"I'm sorry," he said again. "If I ever come across something like that again, I won't butt in unless the female really seems like she needs help."

I pursed my lips and squinted at him. "Okay. Then, I forgive you. Thanks for trying."

He chuckled and walked around me. I watched him go further into the gym before walking out to my truck. I couldn't help being a little shocked that he'd been so willing to admit he'd done the wrong thing and tried to see things from my point of view. A rare commodity in a man. Good for him.

As soon as I closed the truck door, I called Beth and put it on speaker, turning the air up full blast. "Hey, friend!" she chirped. Ever since she'd started a relationship with her new boyfriend, Maddox, also a Kingston, she'd been in a perpetually cheery mood.

I ran down the events at the gym. Beth didn't know Nick, as she hadn't gone to high school here in Black Claw, but she sighed when I told her what he said. "There was one of those guys at every high school," she said. "And they all sucked."

"Agreed," I said, then went into what the mysterious Kingston had done. "He looked like he could be Maddox or Axel's brother. Dark hair, tall, strong jaw. Honestly, he was hot."

"Did he sort of growl and glower?" she asked.

"Yes, how'd you know? His voice was totally deep and grumbly."

"Sounds like Rico. He's Maverick's cousin from Arizona. He got into some trouble a while back and has been living here in Black Claw and getting his head on straight."

I whistled through my teeth and pulled out of the parking lot toward home. "Those Kingstons have no short supply of hot men."

"That's the damn truth," Beth said.

"I was a little surprised he got in the middle. Doesn't seem like a very Kingston thing to do."

Beth chuckled. "Rico is an odd one for a Kingston. He's a little wilder than the rest of them, though from what I can tell he's a good person. Just not as uptight." She giggled. "Maddox would be so mad if he knew I called him uptight."

We chatted on the way home, but even after we hung up, I couldn't get Rico off my mind. He'd been kind, especially after I pointed out the error of his ways. He listened and changed his tune instead of getting mad and defensive.

But it had been my experience that people were kind right before they let me down. I didn't trust anyone, least of all kind people. Why should Rico Kingston have been any different?

Chapter 2 - Rico

First the bar, now the gym. I needed to move out of Black Claw before I ran out of places to go. I hadn't wanted to meet her. I'd avoided finding out who she was. I hadn't even wanted to know what she looked like.

Too late now.

My bad mood had followed me around from the moment I sensed Kara at the bar. Days and days of feeling sour and out of sorts had taken its toll on me, and the blaring radio was doing shit all to help. I smacked the off button on the console. I wanted to tear someone's head off. I wasn't too particular about whose. Maybe that asshole at the gym? He seemed good at making himself a target, especially hers.

The thought of being anybody's mate was laughable. Least of all a woman who clearly needed no help in life. What did she need a mate for?

I hadn't fooled myself into thinking I wouldn't run into her eventually. That was an inevitability. But I also hadn't expected to see her at the gym, of all places. I'd never scented her there before, so I figured it was a good place to work off energy.

My family had a gym at the manor, of course, but going to the one in town gave me some time to breathe. Some Rico time. That worked out well.

A woman with spice is good for a relationship, idiot.

Valor didn't think much of me. He disagreed with nearly everything I'd ever done, including the decision to stay away from Kara.

Whatever. He was welcome to think whatever he wanted about me. No way I was heading down that road. We'd already made too many bad decisions and landed ourselves in hot water one too many times. It was time to keep my nose clean and to the grindstone, or whatever the expression was. I had to keep out of damn trouble.

I parked my truck in the barn beside Maddox's, slammed the door, and trudged across the freshly mowed front lawn and into the house. As I put my hand on the front doorknob, I knew I was in trouble. I smelled and heard my grandfather and Uncle Perry inside.

Great. If they were here, I'd done something else wrong. I had no idea what, but there was no other explanation.

After sucking in a deep breath, I opened the door and tried to act excited to see them. Normally it wasn't that hard, but I really wasn't in the mood for it today.

Gramps and Perry stood with Uncle James, my cousin Maverick's father. It was his house I'd been staying in. If this massive place could've been called a house.

"Rico, my boy, come sit down." Uncle James beamed at me. He'd been amazing since I came to stay with him. He'd opened his home and did his best to let me know I was welcome and loved. But I'd been here a few months now, feeling like the other shoe was about to drop. I'd expected this meeting to happen right after I'd come to Black Claw.

Well, time to get it over with. I walked across the big, spacious living room and sat between Uncle Perry and Gramps, the couch protesting under our combined weight. "What are you guys doing here?" I asked politely.

"We're here to check on you," Perry said. "James has been concerned."

I looked at James with my eyebrows raised. "He has?"

"I've been trying to push you toward finding a job or going to school," he said. He scratched at his cheek thoughtfully. "But you don't seem to be taking the bait. My brother and your grandfather decided to fly in so we could talk to you about your options."

Options? I shifted uncomfortably under the implication. I'd be getting my trust fund soon, then I could do exactly what I wanted to do. Hide away up in the mountains far away from everyone and pretend I didn't have a mate roaming around the world without me. Being alone was my best chance at staying out of trouble.

"We'd hoped that spending time around your cousins would give you a sense of urgency to settle down," Grandfather said with a sound of disapproval.

I cringed. Ah, yes. My cousins. They were likable enough, but they had it all figured out. Life, school, mates. I would've had it all figured out if I'd lived here, too. They'd had easy lives, for the most part. Not like me.

Maybe I was a little jealous. Who could blame me?

Uncle Perry leaned forward. "It boils down to this, Rico. We're giving you a six-week trial. You have six weeks to find and keep a job. You have to find it outside of family connections. If you keep it, you'll still get your inheritance."

Okay, that didn't sound so bad. Six weeks would still put me before my twenty-fifth birthday and the release of my inheritance. I was relatively sure I could make that work.

Uncle James held up one finger. "With a caveat."

Of course. There's always a catch, isn't there? I picked at the fashionably worn spot in the knee of my jeans, waiting for him to drop the other shoe.

"You can have the inheritance, but as an allowance only. You must keep a job for six months, and then you'll get half your trust fund. After a year total, you get the whole fund."

A year. Another year of being a good little dragon before I could escape. I felt like I was watching a trap close around me. It was suffocating.

"You had a job with Stefan at the body shop," James said with a severe look in his eyes. "But after you got a couple of paychecks, he said you started calling out or coming up with excuses to miss your shifts."

James stared at me. As I was an alpha, he shouldn't have been able to make me feel cowed.

Shouldn't have didn't mean shit when my uncle was giving me a look like he was completely disappointed in me. "Yeah, I guess I figured I'd made enough to tide me over until the trust fund kicked in," I mumbled.

"The more you prove yourself, the better this will go for you," Perry said. He put a heavy hand on my shoulder and squeezed. "Kingston dragons don't shirk their responsibilities. Being a dragon is a great gift. We won't sit by and let you waste your life."

Anger began to prick at the back of my neck. What did they even know, anyway? I wasn't wasting anything. What was the point of being a dragon shifter if we didn't enjoy life at least a little?

"You can't take a 'fake it until you make it' outlook with this, Rico." My grandfather stared into my soul. He knew exactly what I'd been thinking. That I could play nice for six weeks, and then six months, and then a year. One year and then I was free. Damn it, I could do this. I needed to.

"Your parents left you a considerable amount of money," James said. "Part of it is the normal Kingston fund that we all get, but as you know, your mother's family had old money from finding oil years ago. She left it all to you."

I didn't like talking about my parents. "I know," I said uncomfortably. The anger I'd been feeling grew deep inside. They wanted to order me around, but they'd all grown up with parents, with loving moms and dads. They hadn't been robbed of their childhoods. Who cared if I wanted to go a little wild now?

When I turned twenty-five in a few months, I was supposed to get my inheritance, then I could be alone and away from everyone's expectations. Finally.

"This is ridiculous," I said. I tried to control my voice, but the rage deep inside me tried to bubble out. "So I got into a little trouble? That doesn't mean I don't deserve my rightful inheritance. It's not your money to control."

Perry and my grandfather exchanged a glance over my head. They'd raised me, along with my grandmother, after my mother and father had died. They hadn't been bad, but there was no substitution for real parents.

Dragons weren't supposed to die in car wrecks. But my parents had. It had rained, but only a small bit, just enough to make the roads a little slick. They were on their way home from a date night and the car slid off an embankment. I never knew if my father was drinking and driving or if it had just happened, but the pack had investigated and hadn't found any sign of foul play.

When they went off the embankment, the fuel line snapped. The car exploded before they could get out of it.

I was told they'd died quickly. I was old enough to carry the memory with me. To this day, I had the occasional nightmare about Uncle Perry coming into my bedroom and waking me up to tell me about my parents. My life hadn't been the same since.

I'd also been old enough to know how good they were as parents. They'd been wonderful. Loving and attentive. I would've had just as charmed a life as my cousins if they hadn't died. I had them in my life for a decade, and it wasn't nearly long enough. Not by a long shot.

But the hard truth was that they *had* died. And instead of having my amazing mom and dad, I had money. Too bad money couldn't hug me or tuck me in at night.

"Do you think your parents would be proud of the person you've become?" James asked quietly.

My anger evaporated instantly. He was absolutely right. They would've been embarrassed to say I was their son. Now that I thought about it, I was embarrassed, too. I stood and took a couple steps away, running my hands over my head.

"I don't mean to hurt you, Rico," James whispered. "But you're a Kingston. It's time you lived up to that name. Is this the legacy you want to leave behind for future generations? What if you have a son someday? Do you want to have to explain to him why you did the things you did in your youth?"

James held my gaze. He wouldn't let me look away or cower.

Perry got to his feet and put his hand on my shoulder. "He's right. We coddled you, doing anything we could to help you forget your pain for a little while."

I thought about my childhood after my parents died. Perry and Gramps had spoiled me, buying me gifts and letting me do pretty much whatever I wanted. Grandma too. But still, it didn't make up for not having my parents. I would've given back every dirt bike and video game system a thousand times over to have my parents back.

My soul felt heavy inside my chest. They were right. I wasn't someone I would look up to. I wasn't even living, not really. I just wanted to get by, day to day. The future was a word for other people. I didn't expect a good future. Just more getting by.

I tried not to let my emotions show on my face when I turned back to them. They'd cut me close talking about what my parents would think of me.

Gramps's face looked as miserable as my own. So did Perry's. They hated knowing I was in pain. At least I knew I had them. They cared.

To my surprise, Uncle James looked just as forlorn. "I'm sorry, Rico. I'd give anything to have my brother back. He should've been here to raise you and love you."

I nodded, unable to reply.

Perry cleared his throat and stepped back. "You've got six weeks to find a job, then keep it until the six-month mark. If you don't follow everything we tell you, and meet all the timelines, your inheritance will go to charity."

I hung my head. I wanted to be a man that they and my parents could be proud of, but I still wanted my inheritance, too. "Okay. I'll do my best."

Not that I had a choice. I tried not to feel backed in a corner, though that was where I was. My emotions bubbled up inside me. "I need a moment alone," I said. "I want to go shift and talk this through with Valor."

Gramps stood. "Of course. Go. We know this is a harsh ultimatum we've given you. Some of this is our fault. We babied you for too long. Shift and find your center."

Ugh. Gramps was all about meditation bullshit while shifted. Valor and I agreed on that one. It was a load of horse shit.

I nodded and stuffed my hands in my pockets as I hurried out of the living room and through the kitchen. By the time I got to the woods, I'd stripped out of my clothes.

Valor took over and launched into the air, rising above the trees and taking us toward higher elevations.

They're right. You act like a child.

Great. Now he was going to lay into me, too. I wasn't a child. I just didn't want a conventional life.

It would've been fine, living alone up in the mountains, until we found her.

He thought we were destined to be with her. I wasn't so sure. I felt the urge, of course. The pull made me want to encourage Valor to alter course and fly straight to her house and claim her immediately.

But of course, we couldn't. I had to be strong enough to hold him back at all times.

Right now, I needed to clear my head and figure out where I could find a job. I only had six weeks to find one in the tiny town or it was bye-bye inheritance.

One way or another, I'd be getting that job.

Chapter 3 - Kara

I'd been holding the flashlight for my adoptive father for nearly a decade, and I would happily do it for a decade more. I was one of the rare foster care success stories in that I'd finally been adopted at sixteen. They were still my family, even though I was nearly twenty-five, and always would be.

Not long after the adoption was finalized, my adoptive mother and father had gotten a divorce. I hadn't wanted to leave Black Claw. My foster homes had all been in Black Claw for the last several years, and I liked the school for the most part. When I asked to stay with Ash, my adopted father, Misty, his ex, had taken off and never looked back. After that it was just me and Ash and his younger daughter, also adopted. She'd gone back and forth between the two houses, but then she'd lived with Misty longer and was far more attached to her.

For me, though, a lot of the time it had been just me and Ash.

"Hold it higher," he said from underneath his truck. He'd always loved putting classic cars together and taking them apart. He started teaching me how to fix them the very first week I came to live with them. I helped because I really enjoyed the one-on-one attention, something that was lacking at my previous foster homes.

Soon after that, he remodeled and turned the

garage into a big bedroom for me. That began my love of all things construction, because he let me help with every step of the remodel.

He wasn't normally one for long, drawn-out conversations. He showed his feelings by actions. Having me help on the remodel project had been his way of connecting with me. And it had worked. I loved the work. But still, even though Ash wasn't an overly chatty person, he was being awfully quiet even for him.

"Why the silent treatment?" I called down through the engine block.

The clanking of his wrench paused. "No reason."

I let him work for a few more minutes, only the sound of metal clanking on metal hanging between us, then I hung the light on the engine block before grabbing his spare creeper. I slid under the truck beside him. "Seriously, Ash. What's going on?"

He sighed and turned his head my way. I smiled at the smudge of grease on his cheek. Grease had been a way of life since I moved in here. I'd moved out a few years ago, but still the grease remained.

Ash rolled out from under the truck, so I followed and sat up to stare at him as he got up and cleaned off his hands. "I heard about the gym," he muttered. He tossed the now dirty rag back on his workbench, but kept his eyes averted.

Ah. I should've guessed. Nobody knew how to keep their mouths shut here in Black Claw. "Yeah, so?"

"I hate you going on these jobs alone. What would I do if something happened to you?" He set his gaze on me, that dad-stare that made me squirm in discomfort.

"I'm fine, Ash." After a quick eye-roll, I hopped off the creeper and took his hand. "I'm not in any danger. Besides, I always have my pepper spray in my belt or bag. I'm careful."

"I'd feel better if you hired someone," he said. He squeezed my hand, imprinting his worries for my safety there. "You're successful. Become a manager."

That had always been my plan, but I still didn't want to stop working myself. "I've been thinking about that, actually. But I've only had my little business going for two years and only recently have I started becoming busy enough to consider taking on a part-timer."

"It's not just having someone to help you or go with you on jobs," he said. "I worry about you exhausting yourself. You're young. You shouldn't be working so much that you can't go out and have a little fun."

Hiring someone to help wasn't the worst idea, but I wasn't ready yet. I'd appease the old man, though, at least to get him off my back. "Okay. I'll hang up a sign at the office."

Ash beamed at me, the grease on his cheek creasing into the wrinkle there. "It's not that I don't think you're capable. I trained you!" He puffed out his chest proudly. "I know you're damn good."

"Of course I am." I laughed at him and handed him a clean rag. "Now wipe your face, old man."

We had a nice visit. I made us some lunch while he cleaned up the mess he'd made in the garage, then I had to go stop by and pick up a part for a stove I had to fix at my friend and biggest client, Abby's rental houses.

By the time my sister, Melody, texted me, I was ready to call it a day.

Drinks tonight. Meet me at the bar at 8. No excuses.

It was Friday night. Why shouldn't I go out? I checked my app and made sure I had no appointments booked in the morning, then blocked myself off. If anyone tried to schedule anything, it would put me down as busy. Then before hopping in the shower, I sent a text to my best friend, Beth, inviting her along. She replied she was in as long as she could bring her friend Abby.

The more the merrier.

I sent that text, then started getting ready. I'd been feeling a bit lonely lately. Maybe I'd finally come across good one-night stand material at the hole-in-the-wall bar in Black Claw.

Yeah, right. It hadn't happened yet. It wasn't likely to happen now. Still, skinny jeans and a button-up might fool someone, and it was a far cry from my baggy work clothes. I shrugged and went with it.

Knowing full well I planned to drink, I called a rideshare to take me to the bar, then scheduled one for later in the evening to take me home. I wasn't sure if Beth and Abby planned to drink, but I knew Melody would. We'd both probably end up at my place, passed out. By the time I pulled up, the place was already pretty busy.

"Hello!" My three friends were already there, as well as Abby's sister, Harley. "Nice to see you," I said warmly. We'd been to a couple of girls' nights together but hadn't really bonded otherwise.

"I hope you don't mind me crashing," she said. "But I had to have a moment without kids or men. They're worse than a pack of dragons."

Abby and Beth burst out laughing. Melody and I gave each other a confused look when they laughed harder than the joke warranted. "No worries," I said. "I love a full table at girls' night. Besides, all of you are dating Kingstons, so hopefully no guys will bother us."

Melody looked at my friends, who she'd only met a few times before. "All of you?" she asked, incredulous. "I knew about Beth and Maddox, but wow."

Abby nodded. "Yes, I'm engaged to Jury, and Harley is with Stefan, who is an honorary Kingston."

Someone started up the old jukebox again, so we had to speak loudly to be heard. "So what's new with everyone?" Abby asked. "Kara? Anything with you?"

I shrugged and shook my head. "I'm thinking about hiring someone, but that's no big deal. I'm really just trying to keep my dad happy."

Melody clasped her hands together and gasped. "You should!"

Beth nodded emphatically. She knew exactly how busy I was. "I agree," she said in a near-yell. "You've barely had time to get everything done. I know there are a few less important jobs pending at the houses, too."

Shit. I'd forgotten about those. One of her tenants tripped and knocked a small hole in the wall with her cane. I would've thought they were lying and had punched the wall—I'd seen that happen all too many times when tempers went up—but the woman was in her seventies. She was just lucky she didn't break something.

"Even if you just hire an assistant," Beth said. "You need someone. You could try to find a woman!"

I hadn't thought about that, and I found myself enjoying the idea. "That would be cool. I could try to make it a company of women."

Everyone agreed that I needed help, and they talked about knowing any women who might want the job. "But I don't really have time to train anyone," I mused. As much as I would've liked to, it wasn't possible at the moment. I shelved the idea for now.

The drinks kept flowing and by the time we were interrupted, I was pretty tipsy. A bunch of men appeared at our table. "We've come to drive the beautiful ladies home," Jury said as he beamed down at us. Abby jumped up and threw her arms around his neck. They pulled over a few more chairs until the table was overly crowded with everyone.

"Hey, now," I said grumpily. "This is supposed to be girls' night."

"It still is." The mysterious unnamed Kingston from the gym pulled up a chair beside me.

Melody leaned over me and stuck out her hand, stars in her eyes. "Hello, I'm Melody. Have you met Kara?"

Rico shook her hand as I tried to avoid looking at him. "Yes, Kara and I met at the gym earlier this week."

"Last week," I corrected him. We'd met at the gym Saturday of the week before. "Technically."

He gave me a quizzical look, but I turned my head quickly. It occurred to me that that might've seemed impolite, but I wasn't in the mood to become another of the Kingstons' conquests. The Kingston invasion of girls' night had soured my mood a bit.

Melody kept trying to initiate conversation with him, but he wasn't biting. He wasn't rude, exactly, but he gave concise, polite answers to any questions. I knew she thought he was hot and considered offering to trade seats with her, but I wasn't sure if I trusted myself to stand just yet.

"Hey, Kara," Beth said. "I may know a certain muscly man who is looking for a job."

I smiled and straightened up, ready to have a conversation other than the one in the middle of Melody and Rico. "Cool. You'll have to tell him to come by the office."

At first, I'd run everything out of my rental house, but after a while I was overrun with parts and tools that I'd been accumulating over the last two years. When a small room had opened up in the short strip of shops beside the grocery store, I jumped on the chance. It would've been better to have been down by the hardware store, but in Black Claw, any space in town was a hot commodity.

I waited for Beth to say something else about the person she knew looking for a job, but Rico leaned forward. "You look nice," he said awkwardly and a little too close to my ear. Beth gave me wide eyes and nodded her head slightly toward Rico.

My mood soured further. Fucking hell. I needed another drink.

A server walked by with a tray full of shots. "Oh!" I called. "Over here!"

After buying a round for all the girls and knocking one back as fast as I could, I turned to Rico and raised an incredulous eyebrow. "I look nice?"

He nodded almost hesitantly. "Yes, the only time I've seen you, you were in work clothes. I just wanted to compliment you."

Why did men think all we wanted were compliments? Still, he was trying to make conversation and be nice. "Thank you," I said and knocked back another shot.

"Sure. I mean, I almost didn't recognize you," he said with a chuckle. "Out of your work clothes, that is."

"Oh?" Where was he going with this? I was trying not to get offended, but he'd seemed at least kind before. Was he going to end up being just like all the other assholes? So much for my optimism for the night.

Across from us, Beth was subtly trying to catch his eye to stop him, but his attention was pretty well focused on me.

"Yeah, you were cute before in that flannel and the belt, but now you look like a..." He seemed to stumble a bit as his words made me more and more uncomfortable, and the expression on his face made me think he only just realized where he'd been going with that. "Real nice. You look really nice," he concluded lamely.

"You were about to say I look like a...? What?" I knew exactly what the fuck he'd been about to say. Beth and Melody both winced, already knowing what was coming.

"Nothing," he exclaimed. The song blaring out of the jukebox went off and the word ended up sounding like a cross between a shout and a scream. We drew some looks from the bar, but I was past giving any shits.

I looked at him with my eyebrows raised, the two shots I'd taken beginning to loosen my tongue. This couldn't be good. "I'm not my clothes, you know." I'd lost all ability to control my tone of voice. I was trying not to be a total bitch but couldn't really tell how I was coming across. "They don't define who I am."

At that point, I was ready to let it go and move on, but damn, Rico had to get in one more word. "Sorry." He didn't sound at all sorry. "I just meant you look all feminine and like a lady."

As opposed to when I was in my work clothes when I looked like a man. Wow. So much for that understanding act at the gym the other day. This guy could go screw himself. "Well, at least I'm lady enough when I want to be, and at the same time man enough to hold down a real job."

I hadn't missed the hint that Rico was the one after a job. And by the look on his face, my words had the effect I'd hoped. His face shut down and he glared at me. The entire table had gone quiet at our exchange.

My phone beeped, distracting me from waiting for Rico to retort. It was already time for my rideshare. "That's my ride," I said. "It was nice seeing you all." I wobbled slightly as I stood. "Melody, are you coming with me?"

Melody's eyes whipped between me and Rico, but I didn't give him the dignity of looking at him.

"We can take you home," Jury offered, "if you don't have a ride."

Melody shrugged and looped her arm through mine. "I'll walk her out."

We walked together and I wasn't drunk enough to miss the fact that we both wobbled as we crossed the bar. "Are you okay?" she whispered. "I'll come with you if you want."

I squeezed her hand in what I hoped was a comforting way. "No, it's okay. I just want to go home and sleep."

After a long hug, she whispered that I should call her if I needed her, and I left in the back seat of a small sedan.

It wasn't until I got home and crawled into bed

that I let the tears fall.

I just wanted to be judged on my abilities and *not* judged for wearing work clothes. Why was that too much to ask?

Chapter 4 - Rico

Saturday was a complete bust. I got up bright and early and hit the town, going to all the stores on Main to look for a job. I even tried the damn grocery store and gas station.

Nobody was hiring, and the ones that were needed skilled trade. The only thing I was skilled at was getting into trouble. Hell, I managed to do that even when I was actively trying not to. A couple of the places, the managers had been female, and it was painfully obvious they just wanted to flirt or get close to a Kingston. No way I was mucking out horse stalls just to be harassed all the time.

And Sunday I couldn't even try to find a job. Black Claw shut down on Sundays. Always had. I'd sat around the manor on my laptop trying to think of places to apply. Everything came up with a big negative. The best photographer in town wanted an apprentice, but I couldn't have them go through the trouble of training me just to quit in a year. That would've been shitty when someone else could've been learning that skill to actually use the rest of their lives.

I wanted to get my inheritance and move on with my life, but I didn't want to be a total garbage person. The guys I'd gotten into trouble with, they were real losers. Hanging with them taught me more than my uncles realized. They taught me exactly what

I didn't want out of life and who I didn't want to be.

So, at least something good came of that time.

My phone beeped as I got out of the shower, dreading hitting the streets again on a bleary Monday. Everyone hated Mondays, so I worried nobody would want to hire me if they were already in a bad mood. Maybe I should grab a bunch of coffees to take around with me or something. Coffee made a good bribe, right?

The notification was a text from Jury. **Got a lead on a job.**

I replied quickly. **I'll take it but keep it to yourself. They said I couldn't use family connections.**

He replied several minutes later as I tugged on a nice-looking pair of jeans. I couldn't bring myself to wear suit pants or slacks. No jobs that would hire someone like me would be that fancy.

No connections. I saw a sign in a window.

He followed it up with an address. It was right on Main Street. I knew I'd definitely hit all the places with signs on them Saturday, so this must've been a fresh opportunity.

Damn. I had to hurry.

After making sure I looked nice, I hurried downstairs and slipped out the front door before Aunt Carla could waylay me. If she got her proverbial claws in me, she'd make me take the time to eat breakfast. I didn't want to miss out on the job because somebody else got there first.

Dark clouds hung low in the sky and it looked

like they could open up at any minute. The town itself was still pretty sleepy, with most people either already at work or not ready to get out and about yet. I got to the shop quickly without any traffic bogging down the roads, but already there was an 'Open' sign lit up in the window. Craning my neck, I peered through the front truck window to see if there was a shingle hung, but nothing told me what kind of business it was. Damn. The only sign was the one that said 'Help Wanted' in the window, and the windows had a reflective tint keeping me from seeing inside.

Well, the worst that could happen was another rejection. It wasn't like I hadn't heard those all weekend. Might as well go in and see what sort of place it was.

Valor stopped me before I opened the truck door. *Find Kara after and apologize.*

As I had since the moment we'd left the bar, I ignored him. He'd totally disagreed with letting Kara leave without clearing the air.

In a way, she'd been right. Kara was gorgeous in her work clothes. What I'd meant by my words that night was that she looked just as beautiful in dressier clothes as she had at the gym, but I'd been trying to be all casual and not make a big deal of it. If her expression was anything to go on, it had backfired big time.

It wasn't like I was in any position to have a mate right now. Besides, she'd said some hurtful things herself. I deserved as much of an apology as she did. The last thing she'd said was about me not being man enough to hold down a job.

It wasn't that I *couldn't* hold down a job. I just hadn't needed to yet. Until now.

As soon as I opened the truck door, I knew. Under the smell of the approaching rain, Kara's cinnamon scent was plastered all over this building. I looked around the parking lot with one hand on the doorknob and sure enough, there was her scent, invading my senses and making Valor growl with the need to possess her.

I had to remind him that in this day and age men didn't possess women.

I disagree.

I figured I'd just let him think whatever he wanted to. I learned early on it was pointless to argue with him.

Sucking in a deep breath, I stepped out of the truck and strode toward the door of the mysterious business that needed help.

More than once in the handful of steps between my truck and the front door of the shop, I considered turning back. But a job was a job, even if it was working for Kara. And maybe I'd be able to convince her I hadn't meant to be a total dick back in the bar. Possibly.

Valor might've never spoken to me again if I'd turned around and left, too.

After a lot of fast deliberation, and a little encouragement from the cold droplets that started falling on my back, I finally pushed the door open and stepped inside. Kara's alluring scent was so strong inside it was like swimming through her hair or something, and the metallic smell of the tools was almost completely covered up.

Not entirely unpleasant.

The tug in my chest intensified as I looked around at the shelves of neatly arranged tools and building supplies. I'd never seen any man's garage this organized. Point one for the ladies.

I idly traced my finger along one of the shelves. "Hello?" I called.

Kara answered immediately. "Hey! In the back."

I walked across the room and through a doorway. Kara sat at a table with weird magnifying glasses on, using a soldering iron on some sort of computer board. When she looked up at me, her eyes were enormous through the magnification.

It was completely adorable, and also difficult not to chuckle at her.

"What are you doing here?" She tugged the glasses off and glared at me.

"Jury told me there was a job opening in town. I'm sorry, I didn't realize until I got here that it was for you." I nodded my head and turned to leave, then stopped. "While I'm here, though, I did want to say I'm sorry about how it all came out of my mouth, about you looking good dressed up. I didn't mean to imply that you look bad in your work clothes and it escalated in ways I didn't mean for it to." Clearing my throat awkwardly while she stared at me in shock, I waited a few seconds, then nodded again. "Clearly, we can't work together. I'm sorry for interrupting your work."

I moved quickly out of the room rather than staying in the midst of the awkwardness and made it halfway across the front room before she called out. "Wait!"

I froze and turned around. Did she want me to go back to the other room? I shifted my weight indecisively. Stay there or go back? Luckily, she walked through the doorway a second later, relieving me from having to make that decision.

"Have a seat," she said, motioning toward a small desk with a chair on either side of it.

Reasons to leave bounced through my brain like crazy balls, but I did as I was told. Sitting on the edge of the wooden folding chair across from her, I tapped my fingers on my knees, waiting.

Kara opened a laptop and typed on it a few times before looking at me again. She definitely looked annoyed. I stopped tapping. "What is your maintenance experience?"

Damn. Right away, I had to sound like a loser. "I don't have any. But I'm willing to learn, and I'm a really quick study."

She twitched her lips and typed in her laptop before looking at me again. "Previous job experience?"

I shook my head. "Nothing much to speak of. Can I level with you?"

She'd just opened her mouth as if to ask another question but snapped her teeth together and nodded. "Please do."

"When I turn twenty-five, I get an inheritance. I never intended to get a job."

One perfectly dainty eyebrow went up.

Oh, I needed to clarify quickly. I hurried with the rest of what I wanted to say before she made up her mind to say no. "In order to get my inheritance, I have to hold down a job for a year. And I don't mind doing that. I don't want to be some totally useless person who can't fix anything, can't do anything. I got a little experience over at the body shop with Stefan, but a maintenance job sounds exactly like something I need."

She raised her eyebrows and started to open her mouth again, but now I needed to sell myself. "And, I know I'll be leaving the job in a year, so you could pay me minimum wage. Experienced handymen would want three times that or more, and even other apprentices would want more. I don't really need much money, but the education would be worth the difference in pay."

Kara shut her mouth again and gave me an appraising look. "So, do you know how to do *anything?* What did you do for Stefan?"

"I can change oil and tires, stuff in a body shop. I did a good job there, from what I was told. This can't be that much different. I feel as though I'm perfectly capable, but ignorant of the how-to."

Her blunt fingernail tapped at the edge of the laptop. "Why aren't you still at the body shop, then?"

Fuck. I'd told her I'd level with her, and her

demeanor had gone from annoyed to appraising. Everyone always said the truth was the best option. I sighed and blurted it out. "I was late too often, called out too often. I didn't take it seriously."

Her face shut down again. Damn it!

I threw my hands up, holding off her response. "But I am now. I'm dead serious. If I don't do a good job for you and you fire me, they donate my trust fund."

Kara's face broke into amusement as she tried to hold back the laughter.

I couldn't help feeling a little annoyed at that, but I kept my mouth shut.

Finally, she sobered up and cocked her head at me, leaning forward on her elbows and meeting my eyes. "Can you keep your opinions to yourself?"

Valor growled in amusement while I blinked several times as I ignored him and considered if I'd be able to do that or not. "I think so. I'll certainly try."

She snorted, leaning back again. "I bet. I'll give you a shot, but here's how we're going to do it. For the first month, you make ten percent of the job's net cost. So any equipment or parts we have to buy specifically for that job comes out of the total, then you get ten and I get ninety."

I nodded, eager to agree to anything. There were literally no other jobs within a reasonable driving distance. If she didn't give me a shot, I was screwed. I sat forward in my seat, the old wooden chair creaking.

"If you're late, you give up two percent. If you don't show, you give up half the next job and only make five percent."

Damn. She was going to be harsh. But I would be sure not to be late, and I would prove it. "Fine. Agreed."

"Once you learn a thing or two if you go on a job by yourself, it flip-flops. You get ninety percent, I get ten."

I raised my eyebrows. "That's generous."

She nodded. "I know. But if you last that long, you'll deserve it." She eyed my shirt. "Do you have tools?"

I shook my head.

She tutted. "I have enough for now, but I'll make you a list of basic tools you need to own. When you have your trust fund and go off to do whatever you're going to do, you'll want some basic tools in your home anyway."

I kept nodding, agreeing with the politest smile I could muster.

"I'm getting busier and busier as people realize a female maintenance person isn't such a bad thing. But I need you to learn fast. If I keep growing at this rate, in about a month I'll need you to be able to do some calls on your own. Do you think you can handle that?"

I was aware that I was lazy sometimes and didn't want to deal with responsibility, but I wasn't stupid. "I won't disappoint you."

"One last thing," she said with a sigh. "My father has been pressuring me to have some muscle with me, especially when I go to places like the gym.

But I won't have anybody thinking that I'm not the boss. I'm in charge, I'm the expert. You're the apprentice, got it?"

She was worried I'd make it seem like she hired me because she couldn't do the job alone. "I'm here to learn, no matter who asks me. You're the expert." Holding up both hands, I closed my eyes and ducked my head. "Don't worry."

I'd really scraped and bowed and agreed to anything, shocked that she was even willing to consider this. It felt all weird not to be the one to call the shots and say how it was going to be, but it wasn't exactly a negative emotion.

I don't mind submitting to her.

That caught me completely off guard. Valor wouldn't submit to anyone, ever. Not even me, really. If he was willing to let her take the lead, that meant he was a lost cause when it came to Kara.

He was going to be a problem.

Chapter 5 - Kara

Rico had asked to start on Monday, but I had my yearly lady-parts appointment that I couldn't miss. I hated those damn appointments and always treated myself to a nice dinner and something pampering at the same time. This time, I went with a pedicure.

Instead of having him work on Sunday, I emailed him a series of videos I found on a video-sharing app. They covered the basics of various areas like the different types of tools and equipment we'd be working with, and some how-tos on repairing appliances and the like.

If he watched them, then great. It would help. If he didn't, then he'd have to work that much harder to be competent. Totally up to him.

Either way, no skin off my nose. One of the reasons I'd agreed to hire Rico was that I knew I could resist him. He was cocky and proud, no matter the act he'd put on about being compliant and willing to do anything I asked him to. Sure, he was hot, but it took a lot more than being hot to get me going.

And Rico definitely didn't have the other qualities. He wasn't warm or caring; he didn't have a bone in his body that would put me before himself. No dangers of me falling for Rico. Nope.

Even if he was delectably hot. And smelled good, like cedar. Ugh, what kind of weirdo was I? Stop it.

I got to the office right at 9:00, after telling Rico that's when I wanted him there. His truck wasn't in the parking lot, but I didn't consider five minutes or so as being late. I'd give him a few. Maybe he was held up by a tractor or something. That certainly had happened to me before, even in a small town in the mountains of Colorado.

But 9:15 came and went. He was late.

I wasn't even mad. That just meant that the job we needed to go on would be more money in my pocket and less in his. When he walked in at 9:30 with a pinched look on his face, I couldn't help being aggravated. "This is how you start your new job?" I asked. "Now we don't have time to go over the tools necessary for today's job. Here." I thrust my spare tool belt at him as he gaped at me. "I packed your tool belt and mine, and the toolbox we're taking with us to the house."

At least he didn't try to give me a bunch of excuses, though if I had to guess, I would've had to say he'd been up too late drinking. Damn rich boys thinking they can get away with everything. Well, I wouldn't go easy on him around here, and he would learn that quick enough.

He nodded and grabbed the toolbox before I could. I let that one slide. He was here to assist me, after all.

"I'm sorry," he said. His eyes seemed sincere, though guarded. "I won't be late again."

With a sniff, I accepted his apology. "If you want to keep this job a year, you have to take this seriously."

A small flash of annoyance rushed across his face, but it disappeared. "You're right. I'm sorry."

Two apologies. Wow. I was impressed. It seemed like some growth for him.

But when he opened the door for me, I gave him a glare.

Rico just shrugged. "Just being nice," he muttered.

After stowing the box in the truck bed, he walked around to the driver's side. "Want me to drive?"

I stared at him, baffled. I couldn't imagine why I would've needed him to drive my truck. "Why?"

He chuckled. "The truck is awfully big."

My jaw dropped. He literally just had to make an excuse for opening the door for me. What on earth made him think that offering to drive my "awfully big truck" was going to sound any better?

"Are you joking with me right now?"

The smirk dropped off his face as his eyes widened. "No, I just thought you might like a break from driving this behemoth."

With a sniff, I shook my head and climbed into the truck without any trouble. "I've driven this truck since I was fifteen years old. I don't need your dick behind the wheel to get to my next job."

Slamming the door, I turned over the roaring motor while Rico gaped at me and ran around the truck. "I'm sorry," he said rapidly. "I swear I didn't mean to assume anything. Just wanted to offer my assistance. I mean, that's kind of what I'm here for, right?"

"When I want your help, I'll ask for it," I snarled. Aggravated, I threw the truck into gear and may have burned a tiny bit of rubber peeling out. "Can we just get through this job without you pissing me off?"

He mimicked turning a key on his lips as he nodded, then was quiet all the way to the rental house we had to work on this morning. The drive was just long enough for me to cool down a bit and focus on the work that needed to be done. The tenants were at work already, so I used my master key to let myself in.

"You can just come in?" Rico asked as he looked around.

I nodded. "Yeah, and you lucked out for a first job. This place is pretty easy." Now we'd find out if he watched those videos.

"Why's that?" Rico carried the bag and followed me through the small living room and into the kitchen.

"The Parkers rent this place and they're meticulously clean." I laughed as I remembered some of the messes I'd walked into in other places. At least there weren't used condoms lying on the counter. I cringed. "You don't always get that."

"Ah." He set the bag on the kitchen table. "What are we fixing?"

"Replacing a pipe," I said. "Simple enough. Now, hand me the tape measure and pliers." I watched as he opened the tool bag and rifled through it. To my surprise, he pulled out both tools within seconds. "You watched the videos?"

Rico paused in the act of handing me the wrench. "Of course. You asked me to."

I didn't respond as I began the job. "You're going to have to get in here close and watch what I'm doing. I'll explain as I go. I expect you to retain this knowledge because it could happen that tomorrow, I need you to go change one on your own."

"Go for it," he said. "I'll keep up."

Under the sink was a tight fit, but he squeezed in as close as was appropriate, his cedar aftershave—or whatever the heck it was—washing over me. It was mildly distracting, but I managed. When I got into replacing the pipe, I found he was able to keep up far better than I'd expected. About halfway through that job, we got a call from my biggest client, my best friend Beth. One of her least favorite tenants had called with their air conditioner not working.

At least I didn't have to go alone. The guy was a real dick. Beth was working on evicting him, but he hadn't done anything to break their lease, so she had to give him the sixty-day notice she had outlined in her contract. She said she couldn't legally evict him faster just for being a general douchebag.

Too bad.

Unfortunately, when we packed up and went down the street to fix his air, he was home. "Hello, Mr. Parker," I said formally when he answered the door. "We're here to work on your air conditioner."

Mr. Parker ignored me and held out his hand to Rico. "Glad to have you here, son. I think it's a leak or may be low on coolant."

Rico raised his eyebrows and glared at the older man. "You should direct your concerns to Ms. Hannon. I don't know the first thing about fixing air conditioning units just yet."

Parker made a sound of dissent but turned toward me. He explained what he thought it was, but his tone of voice was decidedly frostier.

I could live with frosty. It was annoying that it had taken Rico saying something to get Parker to behave, but at least he was talking to me. Having Rico around might not have been as bad as I expected it to be. Parker hadn't said anything about me not being able to do the job, at least. I'd expected him to.

In the two years since I started my business, I'd dealt with snide comments from men constantly. It hadn't been enough to keep me down, obviously, since my business was still growing by leaps and bounds, but a lot of that had to do with the fact that there wasn't another maintenance business in the Black Claw city limits, and the next closest one had a waiting list a mile long.

Unfortunately, Parker was right. A small leak and easy fix once we ran back to the shop for what we needed. I would've preferred he'd been wrong even if that had meant the job was harder, but that was just my pride talking.

By the time we got him all fixed up, we were

both starving. "Did you bring lunch?" I asked.

I hadn't. I packed my lunch most days but had completely forgotten it, sitting on the counter this morning. Man, but I hated it when I did that.

"No, but I'm starving," he said. "Got something in mind?"

I shrugged. "The diner is closest."

He agreed, so we headed there for a late lunch after cleaning up at Parker's. Thank goodness his job was quick and now over.

As soon as we walked into the door, I knew it was a mistake. Every eye in the place swung toward us. Damn it. They were all interested in who was out with the most eligible Kingston. None of them had ever been remotely interested in me or what I did.

Ah, when I thought about it that way, it made sense. They all wondered what I was doing with a Kingston. It wasn't just that he was here, but that he was here with me. Of all people, I was the least likely to have a Kingston go out for a late lunch with me.

They'd figure it out soon enough and stop staring, so I tried my best to ignore it today. We grabbed an empty booth. Rico slid in across the noisy plastic and looked around. "I haven't been in here before," he muttered.

My jaw dropped. "How is that possible? We only have three places to eat in Black Claw. Four if you count a sandwich from the grocery store deli counter. Here, the ice cream parlor, and the fancy restaurant that's technically outside of town."

The server, a girl I'd known all my life, Cynthia,

came by and took our orders. How I loathed her. If I'd known she was working here, I would've suggested sandwiches from the grocery store first.

Rico ordered two cheeseburgers and fries while Cynthia simpered at him and pressed her boobs together so her cleavage would be more prominent. I struck down the urge to remind her that it was a family-friendly diner. When she turned her eyes to me, I plastered a fake smile on my face. "Chicken salad and fries, please."

Cynthia leered. "Hello, Kara. How are you?"

I sighed. "Fine, thanks."

"Still seeing that woman?" Cynthia beamed at me with her perfect teeth and a perfect dimple in her perfect cheek. Too bad she was ugly on the inside.

I stared at her blankly. I had no idea what the fuck she was talking about. "Excuse me?"

"Weren't you dating some woman from Aurora? I would've thought you'd have moved to the big city by now, where they're more..." She tapped her chin. "Accommodating to women of your particular tastes and abilities." Her glittering smile turned hard. She knew she'd provoked me. She knew it pissed me off.

But no. I was not about to sit here and let this horrible woman bully me. "No. I'm not dating a woman and I never was. And if you want to flirt with my employee, you can do it when he's not on the clock."

Rico's eyes went wide as Cynthia tossed her hair back dramatically. "I'm not flirting." Her tone of voice begged to differ. Then she winked at Rico. Of all the brazen bullshit. I didn't give a shit who he flirted with, though if he ended up going out with Cynthia, I'd lose all respect for his ability to choose a partner.

But I wasn't in high school anymore, and Cynthia was no longer the bully that tormented me. I didn't have to sit here and put up with anything, least of all her snide comments. "Come to think of it, I don't think we'll have lunch here," I said. "I can't trust you not to spit in our food." I stood and looked at Rico, who had wide eyes. "Care for a sandwich from the grocery store?"

He jumped up and pulled out his wallet. "Sure," he said. He threw a five down on the table. "To cover our drinks."

"I should've expected this from a woman with no mother." Cynthia sniffed and pointed her nose in the air as we walked past her.

"Hey," Rico said sharply. "Lots of people grow up without mothers and they turn out just fine. You should mind your own fucking business."

I grabbed Rico's shirt sleeve and tugged him down the aisle. "Thanks," I whispered. "But you don't have to defend me."

He growled low in his throat and bared his teeth. "She offended me with that comment."

We stalked out of the small, cool diner and into the sizzling afternoon. "Fair enough," I muttered. I knew the story of our failed attempt at lunch would soon be all over town but really didn't care at this point. They all needed something to talk about. Always did.

"Let's walk." After all that crap, I needed to burn off the energy. After we got our sandwiches, we walked back and sat on the truck bed to eat. We'd had to park at the back of the diner parking lot, so we weren't in much danger of being interrupted.

"Well, at least now you can say you've tried the diner," I joked as I unwrapped my sandwich. I punctuated it with a fake laugh. Anything to lighten the mood.

He snorted. "Yeah, that's sort of why I was late," he said. "I didn't want you to think I was making excuses, but between my Aunt Carla and all the cooks in my enormous family here in Black Claw, I haven't had a chance to go out to eat much. They always pack a big lunch or invite me to eat. This morning Carla insisted I stop on my way out the door and grab a *quick* breakfast." He rolled his eyes. "My Aunt Carla has become one of my favorite people in the world, but I should've known better. She doesn't know the meaning of a quick meal."

"You were late because you stopped to eat breakfast rather than hurt your aunt's feelings?" Well, color me embarrassed. I'd assumed the worst, but he'd been late because he was being sweet. I was glad I hadn't come down harder on him than I did.

He nodded. "But still. I should've planned for that and gotten up earlier. I knew if she caught me coming down the stairs, she'd make me stop and eat."

I stared at him for a second in shock. Why did I always assume the worst of people? Shrugging, I opened my soda and took a big swig. It burned so good, all the way down.

"That's true. You could've gotten up earlier. But I'll give you a pass this time and I won't dock your pay. You were helpful today, much more than I expected you to be." That was diplomatic. The best I could do right at the moment without resorting to an outright apology.

Shockingly, he blushed and ducked his head. He was pleased to have been helpful. Well, damn. That was cute. I chastised myself. No good thinking that way about Rico. He was my employee. That would complicate things for both of us, even if he was remotely interested.

"What was everyone's deal?" Rico asked in a hushed voice. "At the diner. They were all staring and whispering. Do you get that a lot?"

I'd been trying to ignore it. But he had a right to know. "It's a small town. They just do that. It was partly because you're a Kingston. Partly because they love to gossip. Partly because I'm not the sort of woman a Kingston normally goes out with. I'm not..." I wasn't sure how to describe it, so I shrugged vaguely. "I don't know. But anyway, don't sweat it. In Black Claw, as a Kingston, you should probably get used to stares and stuff."

He took a huge bite of his first sandwich. He'd bought three. "Yeah, I guess I've seen that already. I'm sorry that blew back on you."

Wow. The prince could be thoughtful. Amazing.

Chapter 6 - Rico

Kara and I ended up having a nice conversation. Once I polished off my sandwiches, I gathered our trash and stuffed it into the grocery bag. "I'll be right back," I said. Jogging across the lot, I opened the side of the dumpster to toss the trash. Movement out of the corner of my eye got my hackles raised. I turned to find myself face to face with Cynthia carrying a small bag of trash. She moved in close, her body nearly touching mine, and tossed the bag into the dumpster.

Backing away, I had no clue what to say. Different options jolted through my mind, but I rejected all of them. I got out of her personal space as quickly as I could.

Then Valor took over. He'd never done anything like this, and it took me by surprise. I never would've expected him to speak through me. My voice went low, gravelly, and unbelievably angry.

"It would be wise, woman, for you to stay away from me. And especially stay away from Kara. You're rude and clearly a bully."

I had to fight to take control of my voice again. Valor had never been this aggressive and certainly never forced me to behave how he wanted to before. Defending Kara was enough to bring it out of him. Kara being my—our—fated mate had really become more trouble than it was worth.

Cynthia backed away with wide eyes, nearly tripping over a broken chunk of asphalt. I stepped forward once she was out of the way and tossed the bag in. She didn't say a word, but I couldn't stop myself from glaring and staring her right in the eyes.

She was afraid. Whatever I'd sounded like when Valor took over, whatever she'd picked up, it had been enough to scare her.

Good. Maybe she'll follow my advice and leave Kara alone from now on.

In a way, he was right. Still, I hated the thought of anyone, especially a woman, being that scared of me. I never would've hurt anyone, even a waste of space like her.

Well, not that I wouldn't hurt *anyone.* I'd certainly defend myself in a fight or do what needed to be doing. I wouldn't have hurt someone weaker than me... like a woman.

Damn it, I really did try not to be sexist. But the fact was, I wouldn't hurt a woman, while chances were good that I'd hurt a man. If that was sexist, then so be it.

I walked back toward the truck slowly. Damn it, Valor. Why hadn't he let me handle it myself?

You didn't know what to say.

I could've said it with a bit more tact and without terrifying the woman.

How could you let someone speak to our mate that way? Do you not want to protect her?

Of course I wanted to protect her, but there were certain situations when Kara obviously preferred to take care of herself. If she didn't want me to interfere when a large man was intimidating her, why would she want me to butt in when a woman she already knew was doing the same? I had to control myself, and my dragon, even if I had wanted to rip the stupid woman's head off.

When I got to the truck, Kara eyed me curiously. "I saw Cynthia walk that way but couldn't see if you two interacted."

I grunted and leaned against the bed. "It wasn't a big deal. I just said she should leave both of us alone."

Kara's green eyes twinkled. "I'm sure she'll listen to that."

It took me a second to realize she was being sarcastic. "You never know." I stuck my nose in the air. "I used a very stern tone of voice."

As Kara jumped nimbly off the back of the truck and circled around to the driver's seat, I listened to her laugh. The melody thrummed through me. Damn it.

She'd told me we had two more jobs today, but she drove back to the shop. "You can take the rest of the day off if you'd like. You did well for your first day. Much better than I expected you to."

What the hell? Maybe she didn't want to share all her money with me, but hell, it was only ten percent, and I'd told my aunt and uncle I'd be gone all day. If I came home early, they might think I was let go or didn't do well. "The day isn't finished, though," I pointed out.

"I know, but my last two clients are women and the jobs should be easy enough for me to do alone." She refused to look at me.

Ah. She was embarrassed. I suspected she'd gotten past it as we ate, but seeing Cynthia brought it all back out. "If you're sure," I said. "But I don't mind going and helping out, really. Not because of the money, but I'd like to learn."

"It's nothing big," she said in a slightly higher tone of voice. "You won't be missing much."

Yeah, she'd gotten more embarrassed. I wasn't going to press it further and cause her any more shame, so I reluctantly opened the door.

"I'll see you at nine tomorrow," I said. "Sharp."

She laughed. "Make sure your aunt feeds you early."

I rolled my eyes and got out of the truck before walking over to my own. By the time I opened my door, Kara had already backed out of the parking lot. She gave me a little wave but still hadn't looked me in the eye.

I hated that she was upset over someone as insignificant as that hag. I didn't take any stock in what Cynthia had said, but it was hard to verbalize that to Kara. I didn't want to say something wrong and embarrass her further. I'd just have to hope she got over it overnight and tomorrow could be a new day.

She needed space. Given my plans for when I finally inherited my trust, I could respect that.

I considered going for a quiet drive to waste some time so they wouldn't know I was home so early, but I wanted to watch some more of those videos. I was sure I wouldn't have been as helpful today if I hadn't studied the videos Kara had given me. And I'd convinced her to install the app on my phone that showed what projects were upcoming, so I could see what we were going to have to work on in the coming week and watch videos pertaining to those particular jobs.

It couldn't hurt, so I headed back to the manor. If they asked, I'd tell the truth.

Unfortunately, as soon as I walked in the door, Uncle Perry spotted me. "What are you doing home?" He walked out of the living room before I had the first chance to slip unhindered up the stairs.

I'd convinced myself I'd simply explain and that would be it. But Perry's tone of voice ran through me all wrong. "It's not a big deal," I said. I hopped up the first two steps, still hoping to get away unscathed. Maybe I was a little defensive, but then his next words proved my need to be.

He crossed his hands in front of him. "You got fired, didn't you?"

They assume the worst of you.

I didn't need Valor to point that out. I knew it already. "Damn it, Perry, why do you assume that? Why do you always assume the worst of me?"

"Because you've disappointed me one too many times." His low, sad voice made me growl.

My grip on the banister tightened. "Why can't I be given a chance to prove that I want to be a better person? If you assume the worst at every turn, how can I grow?"

James walked out of the door in the foyer that led directly to the kitchen. "What's going on? Why are you yelling?"

I hadn't realized I had been yelling, but now that he pointed it out, I sucked in a deep breath.

"Come sit down, son." James held out his arm as if to put it around my shoulders. "Tell us what's going on and why you're home early and so easily upset."

Not doing as he asked would have resulted in more arguing, so I turned back and walked into the bright living room and plopped down on the couch. "Being home early was no big deal, really. Kara got embarrassed about something and said she didn't need help for the afternoon. She did say that I'd done a good job and to be there at nine tomorrow."

I fixed James with a glare. "Carla made me late. She forced me to eat."

He chuckled and wiped his forehead wearily. "Son, you've got to deal with that. Carla is going to feed all of us whether we like it or not."

I nodded. "Yeah, I think I'm going to set my alarm for earlier tomorrow."

"What got her embarrassed?" Perry asked just as James asked a question of his own.

"Why are you so touchy?"

I fidgeted with a loose thread on the corner of a cushion. "The answer to those questions is sort of the same. The server at the diner at lunch gave Kara a hard time."

Perry exchanged a glance with James. "About what?"

"Kara is tomboyish. She's not the frilly type," I explained.

James nodded. "I've known her for several years. She's just a year or two younger than Maddox, and I know her dad. Foster dad, I mean."

Foster dad. "She was a foster kid?" That must've been what Cynthia had meant about Kara's mom.

James pursed his lips. "I'll let her tell you about that when she's ready. But she's a good kid, always was. She's just a little plain of dress. Nothing wrong with it." He nodded once as if that settled it.

"I like it." The words slipped out of my mouth unintentionally. Both uncles waited for further explanation. "I just mean that I'm not into high-maintenance women. Anyway, it embarrassed her. We ended up leaving the diner and eating sandwiches on the tailgate of her truck. When I went to throw our trash away, I ran into the woman that was mean to Kara, and something really strange happened."

"What?" James asked.

I hoped they'd understand. Maybe one of their dragons had done the same at some point. "Valor… he sort of took over. He told the woman to stay away from me and Kara both, and the sound of a dragon's voice coming out of my mouth scared the shit out of her. She almost fell trying to get away."

James and Perry exchanged another look, this

time with big grins on their faces.

"What?" I asked. "What's so funny? I'm not smiling."

I didn't see much to be happy about. I'd scared Cynthia to death and learned Valor could absolutely take over if he wanted to. This was a relatively low-key situation. In something highly dramatic, who knew what he might do?

"Son," James said. "Kara is your fated mate. Valor will do damn near anything to keep her happy."

This is true.

I scowled at both of them and raised my voice a bit. "What the hell is it about Black Claw and fated mates?"

My attention was pulled to the doorway behind me, from the kitchen. I'd heard the back door open and shut in the kitchen a moment ago but had ignored it. Maddox and Jury walked in with big sandwiches in their hand. They looked a lot tastier than the ones I'd eaten from the grocery store. If I'd known I'd be home so early, I would've waited and eaten Carla's excellent food instead.

"Yeah," Maddox said. He grabbed one of the empty chairs nearby. "I know they say it's a pack's strength, but seriously? Every Kingston in town that wasn't already married is mated."

"Which was just you and Mom," Jury pointed out.

James and Carla weren't technically fated mates, but they'd been married since they were young and were more in love than most anyone I'd ever known. They didn't seem to care one bit that they weren't fated to be together. I found myself wishing many times that I'd been raised here. Not that I didn't love my Uncle Perry and Gramps or anything.

"That's all it boils down to," Perry said. He leaned his elbows on his knees. "The stronger a pack, the stronger our magic. It makes our dragons able to recognize compatible mates. Otherwise, we might still have ended up with the same women, just without the added benefit of our dragons recognizing they are our most perfect match. I believe that Carla is mine." He smiled. "And I dare any of you to disagree. I'll tell her you did."

The three of us burst out laughing. "We wouldn't dream of disagreeing with that," Jury exclaimed.

When the laughter died down, Jury plopped down beside me on the couch. "Dad, I am curious though, why did you never tell me this was a possibility? Why don't more packs talk about it?"

James shrugged. "I didn't see it as being likely to happen. Packs much larger than our own have not gone through this. It's got to do with our familial bond, our trust in each other, that sort of thing."

Perry nodded. "We haven't seen anything like this back in Arizona, and we're easily three times the size of the Black Claw clan."

That was true. We had cousins everywhere back home. And even still, we weren't the largest pack in the States. And I'd never, ever heard of this happening anywhere else. "Is it possible word will get out and other dragons will try to move here?" I asked.

Perry shook his head. "Outside of those dragons that live here, few know about it. Dragons guard their mates possessively, even when they aren't fated. If we're lucky, it won't get out. If it does, we might have loner dragons trying to join up. But that's just not how it works. They could move into the area and still not find their mate if they aren't in tune with the pack."

"So, I'm in tune with the Black Claw dragons?" I asked, shocked.

James nodded and a smile spread across his face. "You are, my boy. It's why we decided to give you the ability to work for your inheritance. If you hadn't shown personal inner growth, the kind we can't see, you never would've found Kara."

That sucked. I'd never had any intention of staying in Black Claw. The appearance of Kara hadn't changed my mind. Valor might've thought she was perfect, but I very much doubted she had any interest in going up and living all alone on the mountain with me.

And no matter what happened, I was still convinced that was the best way I could stay out of trouble. With or without Kara.

Probably without.

Chapter 7 - Kara

Damn, I hated to admit how handy it'd been having Rico around. The past week had gone so smoothly. No men giving me a bunch of shit. I hated that the only reason they were being polite was that I had Rico with me, though. Why couldn't men just get over the fact that they'd hired someone without a dick to do a job they couldn't do?

Testosterone was a bitch. It'd been a week and a half since that first day when Cynthia embarrassed me to the point that I'd let Rico go home early. And it'd been the most peaceful week and a half of the whole two years since I'd hung out my shingle.

And it was thanks to Rico.

Peaceful as far as customers went, anyway. Things between Rico and me were decidedly less calm. He was either making me boiling mad or turning me on. Or making me blush. Or laugh. There was never a dull moment was the point.

After looking at the a/c unit at the gym again, Rico and I headed back downstairs. The owner was there this time with a nasty scowl on his face. Someone must have pissed in his cereal this morning. He was normally easier to deal with.

"Vinnie," I said with a sigh. "If you'd let me replace that compressor, you wouldn't break down every two weeks. Last week when I was in here, there was a hose leak, but every other time I've had to come down here, it's been the compressor. I can only rig it to work so many times."

His scowl grew deeper and darker. He grumbled something I didn't make out.

Rico stiffened beside me. "What did you say?" he hissed.

Uh-oh. The last time I heard him this pissed was when Cynthia said something about me not having a mother. Luckily, I hated her already, but I couldn't afford for his temper to drive away my clients.

Vinnie swung his glare from me to Rico. "I said, if she had a set of cojones, she would've fixed it already."

Rico stepped forward, but I put a hand on his arm. "Vinnie, come on. At least use a line I haven't heard before. You know, you can always call Stevenson's. He can come to take a look at that worn-out piece of crap you're trying to pass off as an a/c unit."

Vinnie wiped his forehead on a nasty-looking rag. "I called him already. He's booked up. You're lucky you're the only other game in town, or you'd never get a job."

I crossed my arms over my chest and raised an eyebrow. "I get jobs because I'm good at what I do, and I don't need cojones to do it."

His face deepened into a darker shade of red. "I think I'll wait for Stevenson's," Vinnie retorted.

I shrugged, ready to leave and let the bastard call my competition, but Rico stepped forward again. "Hey," he said sharply. "When Stevenson says it needs a compressor, and you've had to pay him for a service call on top of Kara here, then you still have to buy a compressor." He seemed to puff up and get bigger, and his voice had a growling note to it I didn't recognize. Fury took over his features as I watched in amazement.

But before my eyes, he seemed to deflate. "Let's go." He stalked toward the door, then turned to wait for me.

Well, all right then. Now that I knew him better, I didn't mind him defending me a bit. It was kind of nice.

"Fine!" Vinnie called out as I put my hand on the door to leave. His tone was angry but defeated. "Order it. Fix it. Bill me."

I turned and gave him a sarcastic bow, which may have been over the top, but damn, I deserved that one. "As you wish."

When I exited the building into the cloudy day, it was with a spring in my step. The part was expensive, sure. But fixing it would mean Vinnie didn't call me all the time anymore. I would make a bit less money.

Totally worth it to get the gym out of my hair. Not to mention all the assholes inside the gym.

"Thanks for the backup." I was so happy, I even considered letting Rico drive. He'd offered a few more times, and now that I was getting to know him better, I felt he was trying to be helpful. Not chauvinistic.

"Eh," he muttered and shrugged. "It was

nothing. The guy is a dick. No wonder everyone else there is, too. I was just being honest."

"Well, lunch is on me. If we don't see Cynthia's car in the lot, let's try the diner again."

He perked up and grinned at me. "I never turn down a free lunch."

"You've done a great job. Honestly, you've learned more skills faster than I ever expected you to." That was the truth. He'd been a great help, and I felt good about starting to let him work on a few things himself with me observing instead of the other way around.

He puffed up again, this time with pride, not anger. I drove the truck down to the diner, which took all of thirty seconds. We probably should've walked, but eh. "I don't see her car," I said. To be safe, I circled the lot before parking.

"Let's eat." Rico rubbed his hands together. "I've heard their pie is excellent."

This time when we walked in, the only stares were women staring at Rico. The town gossip mill had worked its magic over the time he'd worked for me, and almost everyone knew he was just my assistant, not my lover.

Thus, the women began their salivating over Black Claw's most eligible bachelor.

Ugh.

He frowned and grumbled something under his breath as we slid into the only empty booth in the place.

"What was that?" I asked.

He just shook his head. "Nothing, sorry. Ignore me."

A server I didn't recognize handed us some menus and a couple of glasses of water. When she walked away, I asked again. "If something is bothering you, you can talk to me about it. If you want to, that is."

We'd become somewhat friendly with each other, a step above politeness. I looked forward to the time that we could work amicably beside one another. I knew I'd lose him in a year, but he seemed likable enough, now that I knew him a bit better. He'd been extremely irritable today, though.

Rico sipped his water and considered me. "Okay, yeah," he said. "But you're going to think I'm crazy. Do you ever feel like there are two sides to you? The person you show the world and the person you really are?"

That was not at all what I'd expected him to say. My jaw dropped in surprise. "Wow. Actually, I know exactly what you're talking about. I feel like this every single day."

His surprise at my response nearly matched mine at his admission.

"My guard is always up," I explained. "Because it has to be. But I'm so tired of always being guarded."

He nodded eagerly and leaned over the table. "Yes! I just want to be able to fully be myself."

The server returned with our food, effectively cutting off our conversation, but it didn't stop me from obsessing over it. The subject of being myself was something I tried not to think about all that often because it got me all in my feelings. But damn, it would've been nice to have had someone I could always be myself around. Even with my sister and father, I was always on my best behavior. I did everything I could not to slip up with them. I wasn't overly sarcastic. If I lost my temper, I made sure it was never toward them. They were probably the two people I was most like myself around, but still, I wasn't totally unguarded.

My best friend Beth was close. The more time I spent with her, the more of my natural personality came out.

"I really do understand what you mean," I said when the waitress finally left. Squirting ketchup out onto my plate, I drowned my fries and popped one into my mouth. "What is it for you?" I talked around my fry, which I normally wouldn't have done, but having Rico open up made me feel a bit more comfortable.

"Just that I always have to be guarded and on my best behavior. I made some bad choices in my past that haunt me still." He took the ketchup bottle from me and drowned his own fries. "I'm just having a moment."

"Anything I can help with?" I didn't want to push, but I did want to know more about him. I'd been softening toward him all week. Dangerous, maybe, but necessary for a pleasant work environment. Or, at least that's what I told myself.

"You already helped," he insisted. I chewed my

club sandwich and watched him take an enormous bite of his large burger.

"How so?" I busied myself wiping the drips of mayo off of my fingers while he chewed.

"With the job." He waved his burger at me as he talked. It was kind of cute.

Damn it. I'd thought more than one time that something or another Rico had done was cute or sexy, and that had to stop. He was my employee; he was a good employee. There was no room for cute or sexy or the first hints of flirting.

Damn it. Why'd he have to turn out to be such a good employee?

"I squared off with you before. I have an inheritance."

I nodded, recalling the conversation. "Yeah, but you have to prove you can hold down a job."

"Right," he said around another bite. "Once I get it, I can fulfill my dream of hiding away in the mountains and living as a hermit."

Disappointment tickled my gut. I knew he was totally off-limits, but I hadn't wanted him to be a spoiled brat like some of the kids I'd gone to school with, like Nick. Or my ex, Tye. Ugh. He'd been the worst in high school.

I pushed my disappointment away and reminded myself he was an employee and we worked well together. What he did after he left my employ was totally on him. "Well, keep doing a good job and you'll make it to get your hidden cabin," I said.

We talked about small things like what sort of

house he wanted to build. Surprisingly enough, it was similar to my own dream home. Big and open, lots of space to move around.

My foster homes had all been cramped. When I was ready to build, I wanted a home with not as many rooms, but each room being large and airy. Where the furniture in the room didn't take up so much room that it was hard to walk around.

We finished up our lunch, and I felt silly for thinking we were actually connecting for a moment. As I paid our bill and the server slipped a small scrap of paper in Rico's hand, I nearly laughed.

He wasn't interested in me, anyway, boss or not. I was the weirdo, the mannish maintenance woman. Rico needed a job and was taking advantage of me needing someone cheap. It was nothing more or less than that.

Boss and employee.

Chapter 8 - Rico

Weekends somehow were more enjoyable after a hard week of work. Amazing how that was. I'd never expected to feel so self-satisfied as waking up on a Saturday without a care in the world, knowing I'd worked hard all week.

Huh. Was this what they called personal growth? I think so!

Hardly.

Valor was less than impressed. He'd been giving me mostly the cold shoulder since we started working with Kara. When we weren't around her, anyway. He was a lot livelier when in her presence. But at home, he pulled back into himself, and mostly all I got from him were feelings and emotions. Usually anger, or sometimes frustration. The worst was sadness. That one usually left me in a depression I couldn't shake easily, and it was wearing on my resolve.

I started the day with a huge Carla breakfast, surrounded by half the clan. "Did you plan this?" I asked around a mouthful of pancakes. I gestured around the room with my fork.

She laughed and shook her head, doling out another heaping stack of fluffy goodness. "No, all you hungry mouths just show up. I always have to be prepared."

I knew what she meant. I'd been keeping my

phone close by. Kara had said that emergencies could pop up at any time, and if it was something she thought I could handle, she'd be calling me to deal with it.

After breakfast, I took a long shower, leaving my phone out on the sink counter with the volume on high. When I was finished with that, I plopped down on my bed, feeling aimless.

Funny, three or so weeks ago, a whole day with nothing to do would've been the best possible day. Now, I felt incomplete, like there was something important I needed to be doing.

Eventually, I just dozed. My dreams were hazy and vague, but they somehow left me feeling hollow. My phone's shrill ring jerked me from my impromptu nap.

Surprising how much I wanted it to be Kara. But it was Uncle Perry. He'd gone back to Arizona several days ago. Since he'd been gone, he'd called to check on me three times already.

And this would make four.

"Hello?" My tone of voice may not have been the best, but could anyone blame me? He acted like one of those moms that was too scared to let her kid play, so she kept him off the monkey bars or big slides.

"How's it going?" Even though his voice sounded cheery and friendly, I knew the truth.

"I managed to burn the manor down, quit my job, and break Aunt Carla's leg since the last time you called."

Maybe that was a little *too* sarcastic. Oh, well. "That's not funny."

"I'm sorry, come on." I chuckled and sighed. "I know why you're calling so much, but cut me some slack, man. I'm not screwing up. I don't want to screw up. Contrary to what you all think, I do want to make you proud of me."

"I'm glad to hear that. I won't call as often, okay? But if you run into any trouble or if you just want to talk, you know how to get hold of me."

"Okay. You got it. If anything gets too hard, I'll talk it out with you. I promise."

He sounded pleased as he hung up the phone. It would take a lot for me to call him for advice, but maybe it would get him off my back a little. I'd been telling the truth. I wanted this to go well. And after feeling this listless all day, I didn't want to go back to my former lifestyle, even if I did have plenty of money.

With my skin crawling, I had to do something to stave off the boredom. I shot Kara a quick message. **Okay with you if I go for a hike? I won't have cell service.**

She replied within minutes. **Sure. We won't likely get a call anyway, and I'm not busy. Have fun.**

After a quick thanks, I stripped right in my room. Valor and I had worked on shifting quickly after we'd been kidnapped by some guys that didn't want me to give up my other way of life. If we could've shifted quicker back then, we might've been able to escape them without having to be rescued by the might of the Kingston clan.

It had been so embarrassing. My family had to come to pick me up from the playground for being naughty. Ugh.

But since then, Valor and I had trained whenever possible, shifting, flying, and sparring with Jury's and Maddox's dragons.

I opened my bedroom window and launched myself out of the stuffy room, flying forward with a powerful push of my back legs. I barely felt the heat on my skin, but the rushing wind was refreshing. By the time my freefall really started, Valor would shift us and take off into the woods.

Except for this time, he didn't. The ground rushed toward my face, and I screamed at the top of my lungs. At the last fucking second, Valor took over and shifted us smoothly, arcing upward and keeping us from slamming into the ground.

A little warning next time, and it won't be such a close call.

I had a few choice words for my other half, and I let him have it as he flew us up and over the trees. Actually, there were a lot of words, and some I wasn't quite sure were actual words, but it felt therapeutic to get them out.

As I often did to him, Valor ignored me.

I knew the warning thing was bullshit because I'd never given him any prior notice since the first time we'd ever shifted. He was always eager to shift, and since we'd begun training to shift on a dime, he'd been on point each and every time.

Suddenly, it was a big problem? I didn't think so.

When he had the reins, my thoughts drifted across to him like they did when we were in my body. He could speak out loud or think back at me. He liked to talk aloud, though. Well, usually.

C'mon, Valor! I shouted at him internally. *You know we aren't in a position to be taking a mate. You can't blame me for keeping my distance.*

Strong feelings of betrayal swept through me. He thought I was being selfish and not considering his feelings. He didn't have to say the words.

She's a good choice for a mate. I don't doubt she'd make a good one. But don't you want what's best for her instead of what we want?

Valor continued to ignore me. Of course. But Kara was strong, independent, and resilient. And I was a total spoiled brat. Not at all deserving of a woman like Kara.

We flew over the mountains and trees, and under the scent of pine, I smelled rain in the air and noticed a bank of storm clouds rolling in from the west. I tried to focus on the joy of the flight, hoping it would help cheer Valor up a bit. There really was no other freedom like this. It was intoxicating. The wind rushing past us, whistling in our ears, billowing beneath our wings.

I pitied humans sometimes, that they couldn't do this. It was the most exhilarating feeling in the world.

As we flew, I kept trying to get Valor to see my

side of it. Wasn't it better to be selfless and let her find love on her own? Someone who deserved her. I know I sure as hell didn't. On that, we both seemed to agree, but Valor still longed for her. It was a longing so deep, I could feel it in human form.

By the time we got back to the manor, the rain had started pouring down on us. Valor landed, but instead of shifting back as he normally did, he flopped down on the wet grass and spread out. The rain picked up harder as the storm swept through, but he didn't care. His sadness was bone-deep and made my heart ache.

Rico. Even Valor's internal voice sounded almost without hope. What could I do to make him see my point?

I wish you could see in yourself what I see in you. You have such great potential. With a little application of effort, you've got what it takes inside you to be amazing.

His words made me sad. I appreciated how much he thought I was capable of, but he was wrong. I wasn't anything special. I couldn't even adult properly. *Thank you, Valor. Thank you for believing in me.*

Valor shifted us, but because we'd started from the window, that meant we were in the backyard naked in a rainstorm. I scurried to the little building where I kept a few changes of clothes.

I was hurting my dragon. By extension, hurting myself. For his sake, I had to try to be the man he thought I was. At least I had to *try.*

Even though I was sure I'd fail.

***

The rest of the weekend passed with James and Carla totally babying me. With nothing else to keep me busy, I watched a few videos, then took on some projects around the house. There was a bunch of lumber in the barn where we parked our vehicles. James gave me permission to use it, and with a few videos and some dumb luck, I built Carla a shelf to hold her spices. She interrupted me often to feed me, and James frequently checked on me in the barn. After I finished the shelf late Saturday night, I spent Sunday watching more videos. James was great, popping in often to answer questions and leave drinks and popcorn.

I was determined to be more than muscle. More than my trust fund. I couldn't give Valor what he wanted most, but there were other ways I could make him proud of me.

It was time to make my dragon and my family proud.

When my alarm went off Monday morning, I was already up and showered. I made myself a quick omelet before Carla's feet even touched the ground, and then headed for my truck. It was time to get this week started on a good note.

I made it to the shop a full hour before Kara did. But my time was spent wisely because I organized her biggest toolbox. It was something she'd been complaining that she needed to take an afternoon to do, and I knew she hadn't done it.

Business had really picked up and there were just no extra moments to steal for organization.

The look on her face when she came in and saw what I'd done made it utterly worth it. She thanked me so many times, I had to stop her and remind her that we had a full load today.

She beamed at me. "I'm going to let you take the lead on the first job," Kara told me as we walked to the truck.

"Are you serious?" I couldn't have been more pleased. She had been letting me do some of the work myself, but this would be the first time I took the lead. I had studied the app and our jobs, so I knew it was something to do with plumbing but not specifically what.

When we arrived at the rental house, the reason she wanted me to take the lead became utterly apparent. Her eyes glittered mischievously when she explained the job. The pipes were underneath the house, and it was an unfinished basement-crawlspace combination.

While that meant it was cool down there, it was going to be a dirty, bug-infested job. I tried to get Valor to help me with the bugs, but he still was too upset to respond. If he had put out a little of his mojo, the bugs would have scattered and would not have wanted to come near me.

Unfortunately, that was not what happened. The third time I felt creepy-crawlies over my skin, I had to force myself not to shiver. Even a big, strong dragon shifter didn't like the thought of spiders on his skin.

      That first job went very well, despite the dirt and bugs. It was a simple fix, replacing one pipe, and all those things that could have gone wrong did not. By the time we left for the second job, I had a grin plastered on my face from ear to ear.

      "Okay, cowboy, don't get too excited." Kara laughed as she looked at me out of the corner of her eye on the way to our next location. "This job is going to be quite a bit more complicated. You will need to observe."

      Hell, I didn't mind observing. Not really.

      The week went on much the same way. Every job that she felt I was capable of doing, she had me take the lead, deal with the client, make the repair, handle the invoice, from A to Z.

      By Friday, I realized that I had been observing a lot more than just how to complete the repairs. I discovered a lot about Kara herself. For example, she had a dimple in her left cheek, but only appeared if she smiled a certain way. If she was outright laughing, it did not appear. Only when she gave a half-grin of wry amusement did the dimple show up.

      Of course, I had already noticed her body. Kara had a slender frame and looked like the wind would carry her away with a light breeze. But when we had to start working outside in the heat, and she slipped her T-shirt off, working in her sports bra and tank top, I realized that her frame, while slight, was intensely packed with muscles. I was sure she didn't work out, so her line of work must've kept her in shape. Knowing she was so strong was a turn-on I hadn't expected.

She did mention at one point enjoying a run now and then. I couldn't help but wonder if she would enjoy a flight. For the first time in a while, Valor perked up at the thought and rumbled in agreement.

And as she worked, she talked. She talked about what she was doing. She talked about jobs where she had had similar work to do. She told me about times when jobs had gone very wrong. I laughed alongside her, surprised to find how easy it came when I was with her.

I found I loved the sound of her voice. Maybe in forty years, if she continued talking as much as she had been, I might begin to get annoyed, but for now, all I wanted to do was shut up and listen.

Valor's spirits lifted again when I realized that about myself.

You're coming around.

But I wasn't. As much as I enjoyed being around her, nothing had changed. The only difference was that I knew more about maintenance and more about Kara.

And by the end of the week, I was tortured by the things I'd discovered about my boss—and how much those little things turned me on.

I was horny as all fuck. And she had no idea.

"We're taking Monday off," Kara announced as we drove back to the shop from our last job on Friday. "I have some stuff to do."

Instantly, I worried that something was wrong.

"Are you okay? Can I help?" I asked before I could stop myself and mind my own business.

She smiled at me enough to make the dimple appear. "No, thanks. I only need a bodyguard during working hours." Throwing the truck into park in front of the shop, she turned in her seat and looked at me.

She'd thought I wanted to work more hours or something.

Valor did that weird thing where he talked through me. My voice came out low and gravelly, and somehow sultry. "I'll guard your body at any time."

Her face registered surprise or shock and her mouth formed a perfect O. I realized suddenly that I had leaned toward her, and when the blush crept up on her cheeks, I registered how that might've come across.

And I felt like a complete idiot. "Well, have a good weekend," I said in my totally normal and not at all high-pitched voice and scrambled out of the truck. "See you Tuesday!"

I peeled out of there before she could stop me and cursed myself all the way home for letting Valor take over again. Kara and I had been making progress toward being friends and having the rest of my year pass by pleasantly. Then I had to go make it weird.

After getting so filthy, Carla took one look at me and pointed upstairs. "Don't sit down anywhere. Go take a shower."

Chuckling, I did exactly what she said. As the hot water streamed off my back, I leaned against the shower wall with one hand and picked up my aching dick in the other. I couldn't shake the image of Kara working outside in her tank top, sweat making it cling to her trim, tight body. Before I knew it, I stroked myself several times and bit back a moan.

I wished I'd taken her into my arms and run my hands over her firm muscles, pulling up her tank to expose her dusty pink nipples on her small, perky breasts. Would she taste as good as she smelled?

The next moan slipped out as my hand moved faster up and down my shaft, tightening on my head and pretending the tightness was Kara's sheath as I leaned her over the air conditioning unit with her tools spread all around. Her green eyes were electric with want, her voice urging me on… harder, harder.

My hot cum splashed against the shower wall, and I shuddered, letting the orgasm wane. I didn't want to give up the fantasy yet and tried to keep the image I'd created of Kara in my mind as long as possible, stroking my cock until it began to tingle and tickle instead of feelings of pleasure. It didn't take me long to recover, but immediately after an orgasm, my little soldier needed a break. I took pity on him and finished my shower, thinking about anything but Kara until I got into bed and finally fell asleep.

Chapter 9 - Kara

As I downed my third shot, I was suddenly glad I'd told Rico that Monday was a no-go. Melody and Stormy were already on the dance floor, twisting and writhing in the middle of a group of guys, shot glasses in each hand held high above their heads. I laughed as Stormy pounded one and handed the empty glass off to a random dude beside her. He gave her a bewildered but amused look and stepped to the side to put it on an empty table. Stormy was by far cute enough to get away with it.

Excited as I was for Melody's birthday weekend extravaganza, my last encounter with Rico haunted me. His words rang out in my head like the bells above Notre Dame. I remembered the way his soft lips had offered to be my bodyguard, yet his sultry hazel eyes promised a lot more than just guarding. And that growly voice! Holy crow. Thinking about it again made me dizzy, or maybe that was the alcohol doing its job, but I managed to shake it off just in time for the ladies to come back to the table for another round.

He probably hadn't actually meant it like that, anyway. Most guys didn't. Rico had gotten to know me, and he probably felt all brotherly and protective.

It always went that way for me. I was either one of the guys or a fun little sister. I wasn't feminine enough to be attractive, though Melody, in all her sisterly duties, would kick me for thinking that. I was a jeans and t-shirt kind of girl all the way. It kind of came with the job. I would've hated to bend over to work on something in a dress and heels, flashing my bits to every pervert who walked by.

What would've been nice was someone who could just appreciate the casual look I was comfortable in. And of course, keep their mouths shut about it.

"Hey, mopey, drink up!" Melody pushed another shot my way, her face glowing in the dim lighting as she grinned.

At the bar, Stormy waved down the bartender, her amply displayed cleavage making her a top-priority customer.

I lifted the shot glass to my lips, wondering if it had even been worth wearing the lip gloss I'd thrown on before I got here. Looking at the empty glasses on the table, there was probably more on them than on me now. No wonder guys weren't interested in me. I couldn't even wear make-up properly.

"Hey, what's bothering you tonight?" Melody asked, throwing her arm around my neck. "I thought you were looking forward to spending time with your favorite little sister?"

Before I could stop myself, the words tumbled out of my mouth. "I'm not pretty enough to flirt with." Oh, damn the alcohol. This is why I didn't drink that often.

Melody froze at my side for a moment, then started eyeing every guy in the vicinity. "Who's the asshole that told you that? I'll have his balls."

"Whoa." I laughed, grabbing her before she could make good on that with some poor schlub. "No one, it's nothing. I just…" I sighed and gave in to telling her the truth. "A thing happened, and I'm overthinking it like usual and reading too much into what he said."

"Oh, do tell." Stormy landed on the stool across from us, drinks in hand.

So I explained, doing my best to stick to the facts and not the dreamy way his lips quirked up in amusement, or how his seemingly appreciative gaze looked me over from head to toe, how he leaned in close, or how utterly amazing he smelled. All week, he'd been driving me nuts just being nearby.

The girls' eyes all weighed on me, staring, and suddenly I was self-conscious. Did I misread the entire situation? He wasn't flirting, couldn't have been. Right?

"Honey, you need to stop that right now," Melody admonished, squeezing my shoulders. "You are amazing, beautiful, *hot*—"

I gave her a weak laugh to interrupt her words and leaned into her, the alcohol buzzing warmly under my skin. "No one has ever called me hot before. I'm too much of a tomboy for that to apply."

Melody snorted. "Well, he'd be a damn fool to look over you for something that stupid."

"And every guy in here, too!" Stormy chimed in loudly, raising her glass.

"That's right!" Melody handed me another shot and we clinked our glasses together. "But the point is that you are stunning the way you are, and I'm sure plenty of guys would agree. It's not your fault that you're always around idiots who can't see your true value under jeans and a button-down. Now, get your sexy ass up and come dance with us!" She tugged on my hand and dragged me from the barstool. As soon as my feet hit the floor, I knew exactly how many shots I'd had. I felt them behind my eyes.

My heart swelled with love for my foster sister, even as she smacked my butt through my skinny jeans and led us out on the floor. I let the music carry me away for a few minutes and tried to stop thinking, feeding off of my sister's euphoric vibe. Even so, the dancing didn't last long. I made it through three songs before I felt like I needed to sit down again. I couldn't bring myself to pull them away from their fun, so I signaled to Melody that I was heading back to our table, receiving a thumbs-up in response.

"Hey, gorgeous. Long time, no see."

I jumped and spun shakily at the familiar face as he grabbed my arms, steadying me. Towering over me was a blast from the past I'd hoped to never see again: my high school ex, Tye. We'd only dated for a couple of months, and he'd been my first, making me fall for him and believe he was something he definitely wasn't.

As it turned out, it was all some stupid bet he had going with his jock friends and he dumped me right before prom. All that money wasted on that stupid poufy dress I didn't even get to wear. It was worse than a teen romance because Tye hadn't realized in the end how tricking me had been cruel and figured out he was in love with me.

No, he'd simply been cruel.

"How much have you had to drink tonight, Kara?" he asked, grinning smugly as I pulled away and heaved myself back onto the stool. He helped himself to Melody's seat as his friends took over the rest of our table, adding their beers to our collection of shot glasses and a random martini glass.

"Not enough to be happy to see you," I replied heatedly, though it may have come out a little slurred. Whoops. Maybe I wasn't quite sober enough for this encounter. Damn it.

Tye threw his arm across my shoulders as Melody had a while ago, replacing the safe, comfortable feeling she had given me with a slew of red flags. His friends smiled and laughed at us, and I narrowed my eyes at them. Something about this encounter was making my skin crawl, even more than the average creep would. But my mind was so fuzzy, I couldn't tell what was so off. Maybe it was our history, but even drunk, I didn't trust him as far as I could throw him. I tried to shrug him off, but he held firm.

"So, I've been thinking about us for a while now," he started, leaning in close enough to smell the sour stench of beer on his breath. "About, you know, all the mistakes we made when we were kids."

Mistakes? The fuck? I glared at him, but he ignored it. The prickly feeling on the back of my neck was starting to alarm me and a little bile rose in my throat. "*You* were the only mistake I made, and I don't care to repeat it. Please let me go."

"See," he continued, tightening his grip further. "You were my mistake, too. You were the one I let get away from me because of some lame bet. I think we should try again, make amends and all that. I think you'll appreciate how much I've *grown* since then." His buddies burst out laughing and jeered at me.

With the alcohol numbing my senses, it took me a second too long to realize he'd just forced my hand onto his stiffening crotch. I jerked it away and quickly slid off the stool and out of his grip, mumbling something about the restroom as I headed unsteadily in that direction as fast as I could. Thank goodness I hadn't worn heels. I never would've made it. The sounds of his friends' laughter followed me down the narrow hallway and through the door.

In the relative quiet of the bathroom, I leaned my hands against the sink and hung my head, taking deep breaths. Despite the heat of the bar, my arms were covered in goose flesh. My stomach swirled nauseously. I didn't think it was the alcohol, but I couldn't quite pin it down. It was like my whole body was trying to give me some kind of warning, though if it was about Tye, our past was warning enough. I knew what a creep he was. He was a moron to think he was getting another shot after what he put me through.

I flipped on the tap and splashed cool water on my face, dabbing it dry with the cheap paper towels they always had at these places. Seriously, couldn't they afford something just a little softer? These things were borderline torture devices. One of the stalls behind me flushed and a girl walked out, making eye contact with me in the mirror. I looked away, pretending to straighten my hair. My green eyes were abnormally bright and my face a little too pale, but I chalked it up to the alcohol.

"Sorry, it's none of my business, but are you okay?" the girl asked as she washed her hands, glancing over cautiously.

I started, not expecting her to speak to me. "Hm? Oh, yeah, just needed a break."

The girl grabbed a handful of paper towels and eyed me. "Okay, if you say so."

As soon as she left, I took another deep breath and shook my hands out. They still felt tingly, but I pushed past it, trying to will myself sober again as I walked out the door and smacked into a firm chest. Tye blocked my path, an unnerving grin on his face, and the goose flesh erupted down my arms again. I tried to move around him, but he stepped with me.

"Hey, hold on a second," he said, catching my arms lightly. "I was just trying to talk to you, and you ran off."

"I'm here with people," I pointed out, trying to step away and go around again. "Let me past. I need to find my sister."

He laughed, blocking my way again. "I'm sure she's a big girl who can take care of herself. Now let *me* take care of you."

Grabbing my face, he leaned in, but I just barely dodged the kiss and shoved pathetically at his chest. Normally I had no problem taking care of myself, but I was drunk, and my reactions were poor at best. I watched with growing trepidation as his arrogant face morphed into rage. Panic hitched in my chest as he pushed me against the wall and snagged my arm in a vice-like grip, one I was sure was going to leave a bruise.

"No, stop!" I yelled, hoping someone was close enough to hear. Maybe that girl who cared enough to ask about me in the bathroom was still close by. "Let go of me!" Damn it, why hadn't I walked out with her?

"You don't get to say no to me after what we've done," he purred menacingly, licking his lips and leaning in again, pressing his body flush to mine. I closed my eyes and turned my head, trying to use the wall as leverage to buck him off, but that just seemed to urge him on.

Suddenly, the pressure of Tye's body was gone, replaced by cool air, and a roaring sound filled the hallway around us. I peeked my eyes open to see Tye pinned at the throat against the other wall by Rico's brawny forearm. My heart danced at the sight of his dark brown hair and the hazel eyes that glanced back at me with concern. Or at least that's what I told myself, trying not to overthink things again, especially in my disoriented state. The look he leveled at Tye, though, promised pain.

"Do you not understand what the word 'no' means?" Rico growled, shoving his arm harder under Tye's chin. "Or are you hard of hearing?"

The blood drained from Tye's face and he tried to gasp in another breath before Rico finally released him. He coughed and stumbled a couple of steps away while Rico whirled to me, gently taking my arm to inspect it. Just as I thought, there was already a pretty well-defined red mark that had started to darken. I looked up into Rico's face, and if I hadn't been watching, I might have missed the strange flicker in his eyes. Before I could ask about it, he spun and threw his fist into Tye's gut.

Tye crashed to his knees, wheezing and holding his stomach. I flinched, knowing how much that had to have hurt, but I found I had no sympathy for the sleazeball. I was worried, however, that Rico might go too far and get in trouble for my sake. The look on his face, the tension in his stance, screamed violence, and I found myself stepping toward his back, prepared to stop him if I felt I needed to.

But apparently, I had nothing to worry about. Rico wound up for another blow, then seemed to think better of it, shaking his head as he stepped around Tye. "Come on, Kara," he said just loud enough for me to hear.

I followed closely, reaching out to him, my head swimming. He paused as my fingers brushed his shoulder, a much more pleasant tingle zipping up my arm from the tiniest contact. His eyes traced a path from my fingertips, to the blotchy red mark on my arm, to my eyes.

"Are you okay?" he asked softly, his voice as silky smooth as melted chocolate.

I nodded, but he noticed the slight tremble in my hand and, judging by his reaction, mistook it for fear of Tye rather than gratitude for him. Rico slid past me, back into the hall, and grabbed Tye by the back of the shirt, pulling him to his feet. If the expression on his face wasn't so serious, I would've laughed at the height difference between them. Rico was taller than me by several inches—hell, most people were—but Tye had been tall even in high school, something that helped make him a local football hero. He practically cowered under Rico's *tender* care, though, as he was shoved unceremoniously down the hallway and back out into the bar.

Tye's group of friends stood when they saw us, and Melody and Stormy were already headed in our direction with alarmed looks on their faces. Rico shoved Tye away, so he stumbled and threw a weak glare over his shoulder. We were getting more looks at that point, even before Rico took another intimidating step toward my ex.

"Next time you feel like being a pushy bastard and forcing yourself onto women, think harder," he yelled just loud enough to be heard over the music. I could see people leaning toward each other, pointing at an increasingly angrier Tye. "And if you lay so much as another finger on Kara, you will lose it."

The group of guys gathered around Tye, who seemed to be bolstered by their presence. "You'll be hearing from my family lawyer." He sneered, stepping back into his friends. "You have no idea who you just messed with."

"Oh, yeah?" Rico replied, giving him a smile with an edge in it. "Well, I'll tell you who I am. I'm a Kingston." His smile sharpened. "Do your worst. Just stay the hell away from Kara."

Tye glared even as his friends ushered him out of the bar. Rico maintained eye contact until he disappeared, then turned to me, taking my arm again. He looked at it, smoothing his thumb lightly over the purpling skin there.

"Does it hurt?" he asked, meeting my gaze again.

Speech had all but fled me at the look in his eyes, so I shook my head. There was something primal, something predatory about them, like a hidden side he kept locked away. Though he looked dangerous, I didn't feel afraid, and his touch on my arm was the opposite of how I felt when Tye touched me. I felt protected, safe. Cared about.

Then the word vomit happened again. "You have predator eyes."

My breath vanished when the hunter met my gaze again, and my knees gave out on me. Oh, what was I? Some sappy, moon-eyed princess? But he caught me and laughed huskily in my ear.

"Exactly how drunk are you?"

Instead of waiting for an answer, which I was too embarrassed and maybe a little too lightheaded to give, he grabbed my hand and steered us toward the bar. Melody and Stormy ran up to us, grabbing onto me, asking a million miles a minute different variations of "are you okay?"

Rico leaned toward them. "Sorry, ladies, but I think she's had enough. I'd like to see her home safely."

The room began to feel warm, and I barely heard Melody's stuttered response and Rico thanking her. I grinned like an idiot, and Melody and Stormy both looked worried as they each hugged me goodbye.

"Mmbye, g'night, guys," I slurred as Rico pulled me along.

The fresh air smacked me in the face as he opened the door, but it didn't do much to clear my head. He'd parked close by, and soon I was piled up in his truck with a giddy feeling rolling through me that I couldn't tamp down and wasn't sure how to explain. Some things were best left until the morning to process.

Chapter 10 - Rico

"You're going to break the steering wheel." Kara giggled and hiccupped at the same time. Loosening my grip, I glanced at her out of the corner of my eye with amusement. Drunk Kara had a few different personalities, but this was my favorite so far.

Valor had perked up a bit and having him in a better mood had done wonders to lift my own spirits. He was so satisfied after scaring the shit out of the dick who tried to force himself on Kara that he'd forgotten to be forlorn.

Hopefully, the incident would help him perk up long-term.

I'd originally headed to the bar with every intention of getting Kara *off* of my mind.

That hadn't worked out so well. I felt her pull as soon as I opened the bar door, but then when I stepped in, anxiety washed over me, as well as a sense of duty. It pressed on me so hard, I'd had to find her and fast.

Thank goodness I had. The thought of what could've and would've happened to her if I hadn't come in when I had made me nauseated.

And worse, it made me think about my past.

Not that I'd ever forced myself on a woman. I was fucked up, but not *that* kind of fucked up. But I'd turned a blind eye a few times when a girl had been harassed. If I ever thought a woman was about to be raped, I would've stepped in, but I also never bothered to make sure they were okay.

If I hadn't shown up, and all the other men in the bar had done as I would have just a few months before, what could've happened to my sweet mate? I didn't want to think about it, or nothing would've stopped me from turning around and going back.

I was immature as hell, and I didn't like what I was discovering about myself.

Kara stared at me with her head tilted as worry raced through my mind. What if I didn't ever make it past that guy, that immature, selfish guy? What if I disappointed my family? And Kara?

I really hoped there weren't any repercussions from scaring that guy. He could still sue, even with me being a Kingston, that was no guarantee. He could press assault charges or something.

And that would mean I hadn't kept my nose clean. They could've taken away my inheritance.

They would understand, had to understand. There was no way I could've let that dick get off scot-free. No way.

I was protecting my mate.

"You look like you're holding in something bigger than yourself." Her voice was sing-songy and dreamy.

A loud laugh slipped past my lips. She had no idea what I held back. And Valor was certainly bigger than me. "A lot of people fight inner demons."

She nodded wisely and tapped her nose. "That is very true."

"What are yours?" I blurted, hoping she'd actually answer. Maybe I was relying a bit on her inebriation to get her to open up, but I'd already shown personal growth by not beating that fucker within an inch of his life. Prying for information from Kara wasn't something I could talk myself out of.

She went quiet for a long time. I began to think she'd passed out, but finally, she spoke. "I'm worried I'll become my parents. My biological parents, not my foster father." She sighed, sounding forlorn and worried.

"What's wrong with that?" I asked. I winced, suddenly unsure if I wanted the answer.

The scenery rushed by as she considered her answer. "I don't want to become addicted."

I hesitated, then asked, "To what?"

"Anything. Drugs, alcohol… A person." Her nervous laugh made my heart freeze. Did she mean she didn't want a relationship at all?

Then I had to tamp down my fear because it didn't matter if she wanted one. *I* didn't want one. Not for a long time. If ever.

Valor growled but quietened when Kara continued talking.

"I'm scared I'll develop an addictive personality and latch onto someone who will eventually leave me." Her voice dropped to a whisper and she wrapped her arms around herself. "Everyone leaves me."

Damn. Her pain carried in her voice like a fist around my heart. It was enough to break it into a bunch of small pieces.

I didn't want to push, but my curiosity wouldn't let me be silent. "What did your parents do?" I asked quietly.

Her voice was decidedly more sober than when she'd first collapsed in the passenger seat. "I was put in the foster care system when I was nine. My parents were addicts and pretty much left me to fend for myself. A neighbor caught on. When child protective services came, there wasn't any food in the cabinets. I'd been swiping snacks from the gas station down the road from my house to keep from starving. My parents had been gone for several days."

The pieces of my heart broke again into even smaller bits, but at the same time, my blood boiled with rage. I was glad she was opening up, but my protective instinct was kicking into overdrive and I could feel Valor's undivided attention on her.

"I see them around town occasionally. I'm not sure they noticed I was gone until much later. They don't even recognize me now."

By the time she finished, if I hadn't had excellent hearing, I wouldn't have been able to make out her words. I clenched the steering wheel hard again. She deserved so much better than that.

"This sounds cliché, but it's their loss," I said loudly. "You're the most amazing person... I think I've ever met." The need to hug her was strong, almost enough to make me pull off the road to her house and pull her into my arms.

But we didn't have that kind of relationship. She probably would've thought I was attacking her like the guy in the bar.

Find her parents. We will char them to ash.

I had to remind him that murder was bad, but he didn't lose his anger. Neither did I. We stayed there in that moment with her. She needed us.

When I pulled into her driveway, she was quiet. This time, I was nearly sure she had passed out. I ran around the truck and opened her door, but her hand hung limply beside her in the seat. Yep. She was out cold.

After unbuckling her, I tried to rouse her, but it was no good. "Okay," I said. "Up you go."

Picking her slight frame up into my arms was far easier than it should've been.

And far more pleasurable. I was inundated with emotions ranging from desire to satisfaction at caring for my mate.

Valor was beside himself, trying to get me to sniff her.

I had to tell him to stand down. He was being creepy.

"Hey," I whispered urgently and jostled Kara in my arms. "Keys."

She woke up enough to dig her house keys out of her pocket. I managed to keep her upright and unlock the door at the same time, pushing it shut behind me with my foot.

Her home smelled like cinnamon, just like her. It made my nose tingle in a good way. I propped her up on the couch, then tried to rifle through her kitchen drawers as minimally as I could to get a cup for water and a straw. I found ibuprofen on top of her refrigerator.

"Come here, you." I sat beside her and propped her up, which consisted of her nearly in my lap with my arm around her shoulder. "Take this," I said in a loud voice.

It was enough to get her eyes open. "What are you doing here?" she said groggily.

"Trying to help minimize your hangover. Take this." I shoved two pills in her mouth before she could argue, then the straw.

Kara furrowed her brow, but she pulled on the straw and washed the pills down. "Okay," she whispered. Her head dropped to my shoulder.

I peeked in the cup to find she hadn't drunk much. "No, drink the whole glass. It'll help rehydrate you while you sleep."

Whining was one of my least favorite sounds, especially when women did it. But my experience with women whining had been limited to those that thought it was cute. It was absolutely not cute.

Yet when Kara whined about having to drink the water, it was. I smiled and pressed the straw to her lips again. "Drink," I urged.

She grunted in protest, but she wrapped her plump, kissable lips around the straw and drank.

Damn. I had to look away. Now was absolutely not the time for that.

It took several minutes, but by the time she finished the water, she was more awake and staring at me.

After a tiny burp that reeked to high heaven, she sighed. "You're really attractive. If I was brave enough, I'd tell you."

I was already trying to hold back laughter after the burp. Her words put me over the edge, and I guffawed. "You're beautiful. If I was brave enough, I'd tell you."

As she laughed, she stood, but immediately plopped back down, her legs too wobbly to get her to her bedroom.

"Can I carry you to your bed?" I asked.

She mumbled something I didn't catch, even with my super-dragon-hearing. "What was that?" I asked.

"That way," she yelled and pointed her unsteady arm toward a door on the other side of the living room.

"Aye, aye, Captain." I scooped her into my arms again, to Valor's delight. He purred deep in my chest.

Kara heard it and rolled her tongue in imitation, but I highly doubted she'd remember it in the morning.

I fumbled for the light switch, trying not to bang Kara's head on the wall at the same time. When light flooded the room, I was stunned to see how feminine it was. Every surface was pink and white. Roses covered the wallpaper and her bedspread was mostly pink and white with some purple.

Not to mention the million pillows all over the bed. For Pete's sake. I set Kara down as gently as I could on top of all the pillows, then started pulling them out from under her and throwing them on an armchair—also white and pink—in the corner.

By the time I got all the pillows moved and the blanket tugged out from under her, Kara's eyes were drooping again. She kicked off her shoes and fumbled with her belt.

I really, *really* wanted to help her with it, but if I started that I wasn't likely to stop. She managed to get it unbuckled. I looked away as she shimmied out of her jeans.

Claim her.

Yeah, right. Like I could do that right now while she was passed out drunk. That would've gone over great.

As soon as I heard her jeans hit the floor, I yanked the blankets over her before I had a chance to see anything tempting.

Kara let out a light snore as I tucked the blanket up under her chin.

The bedroom had two doors off of it. I peeked behind each, finding a bathroom behind the second door—and a garbage can. After putting it beside the bed, my gaze caught on Kara's beautiful, peaceful face. She didn't have a bunch of makeup on, but her skin was so perfect it looked like it. Or I just couldn't tell one way or another. Whatever, she was gorgeous.

Her skin was kissable. I longed to brush my lips against it and feel the velvety softness but standing here watching her sleep was creepy enough. Stealing a kiss would've been a violation.

Mine.

He'd been repeating that word and growling for a few minutes.

I didn't mind. I got it. The urge to stay and protect the small woman was astronomical.

With all the willpower I had in my body, I made myself stand up and leave.

Barely.

Chapter 11 - Kara

"You need protein!" Melody yelled at the top of her lungs. Or maybe that was the hangover talking.

I groaned and pulled my blankets further over my head as it throbbed painfully. My sister had turned up at the ass-freaking crack of dawn with stuff to make for breakfast. She'd tried to drag me out of bed, but my headache kept me from following her into the kitchen. The smell of food wafting through the door was making my stomach turn.

"Get up!" Melody's voice grated on me, all perky and cheery like we hadn't both drank half the bar's contents last night.

"Shut your trap!" I yelled back. I curled up tighter under the blankets.

"Come on, I made you my hangover cure." Melody stared at me from the bedroom door. "You know it always works."

Reluctantly rolling out of bed, I had to put my hands on either side of my head to keep my brains from spilling out of my ears. "Yeah, but it tastes like pure ass."

Melody's laughter floated from the living room as she walked back to the kitchen. I looked down at myself. I still had my shirt on from the night before, and my socks and undies, but my jeans and shoes were on my bedroom floor.

I didn't remember taking them off. It wasn't often in my life that I'd gotten drunk enough to black out. I vaguely remembered Rico driving me home.

As I sat sullenly at the kitchen table and watched Melody dance around the kitchen like she'd had her hangover professionally removed, more memories from the night before flooded my brain.

Starting with what Tye did. Oh, shit. I gasped and stared at Melody with my jaw loose. "Rico kicked Tye's ass," I whispered.

She nodded smugly. "He sure did. I didn't see it, but the aftermath was glorious."

"I saw it." Horror and delight filled me in equal measure. "Rico knocked the absolute shit out of Tye." The memories flooded back. Watching Rico destroy Tye's confidence and beat him a little had been the highlight of my week, and I'd almost forgotten it.

"So, what's going on between you and Rico, hm?" Melody asked as she slid sausages off the skillet and onto my plate. She waggled her eyebrows at me and grinned.

"Nothing," I said with absolute certainty. But then a flash of Rico tucking me into bed crossed my mind and suddenly I was less sure. More and more memories pushed through the brain fog. He'd made sure I drank water and took a pain reliever. My hangover would've surely been much worse if he hadn't.

It wasn't like he'd been on the clock. He could've shoved me in the door and took off for home. Hell, it hadn't been his responsibility to defend me at all. It wasn't like I'd hired him to be my white knight at a bar on the weekend. He hadn't had to do any of it.

But he'd defended me, taken me home, then made sure I got safely in bed. And there was even a garbage can beside my bed. Try as I might, I couldn't think of a single second he'd been inappropriate. My memories were a bit fuzzy, but I was pretty sure I wasn't missing any time. He'd been a gentleman right up to the end.

I shook my head and took a bite of the sausage. It didn't matter how nice he'd been, because believing he cared about me would be setting myself up for disappointment. I wouldn't fall for that again.

"I don't buy it." As usual, Melody seemed to read my thoughts. "That boy seemed like a man on a mission." She put the eggs down and joined me. "The way he took care of you and was so protective of you?" I followed her fork as she waved it at me. "It was freaking hot."

Butterflies filled my stomach, but still. I ignored them. He was my employee, and we'd been friendly with each other. "I'm sure it's nothing."

Melody was like a dog with a damn bone. "No. You should test the waters and see what's there. You can always find another assistant, but how often is a gorgeous, eligible Kingston going to fall in your lap? Despite how it may seem sometimes, I'm sure there's only a limited supply of them."

She ate with an air of superiority as though she had the answers if only I'd listen.

I wasn't so confident. "He needs the job," I said around my eggs. "If we try something and it goes wrong, it means a big disappointment for him." It wasn't my place to say any more than that about Rico's business.

"Kara, you might be surprised about how many men are interested in you if you'd stop blowing them off before you give them a chance."

She might've been partly right, but no way I was about to admit it to her. High school, and mainly Tye, had done something to me. I'd dated a few times, but only if the guy had made an exceptional effort, and it had never ended well.

It had also never really ended badly, not since high school. I never let myself get close enough for it to end badly. It was too risky.

Melody tossed another sausage onto my plate. "Invite Rico to my birthday dinner. That way, he'll already be there when you get wasted." She winked and forked up a big mouthful.

I was already mostly full after a few bites. My stomach rumbled, and I knew I'd spend half the morning in the bathroom.

And I had absolutely zero intention of drinking a single drop of alcohol tonight at Melody's dinner. Not after feeling this way.

"I'm not drinking. But I'm happy to be DD," I offered. "I guess a little assistance wouldn't go amiss."

I wouldn't have wanted Rico to think I was using him, or that I was interested in him, even though my feelings had shifted. But maybe he wouldn't mind a free dinner and watching some women act like fools. My sister and her friends could be pretty amusing when drunk.

After breakfast, I loaded the dishwasher and went back to bed for a while. After a nap, I stayed in bed and watched old reruns of TV shows I'd loved as a kid. That was my one escape. Almost every foster home had a television. And none of them had cared if I stayed up and watched as long as I kept out of their hair.

When I couldn't put it off any longer, I dragged my ass out of bed and showered, pulling my hair up in a ponytail. Tonight, I didn't even bother with the lip gloss. Who cared?

Last night it had just been me, Melody, and Stormy. Tonight, more girls ended up at our table than I knew Melody had friends.

And these girls knew how to knock them back. I watched in amazement as they took shot after shot, chasing them with light beer.

Had I drunk that much last night? No wonder I still had a bit of a hangover. There's no way I could've gotten all these girls home.

Maybe Rico would be a big help after all. I grabbed my phone.

You busy?

Melody tried to drag me out onto the dance floor, but I resisted and pushed her toward her friends. She went without much resistance.

When I sat back down, I had a reply from Rico.

Not at all. What's up?

Any chance you'd like to come help me be a DD for my sister's drunk friends?

He responded within a minute. **At the same bar?**

Yep.

To my intense relief, he said he'd be right down. Fifteen minutes later, he walked into the bar, and I had to pretend I didn't notice as I stamped down the excitement I felt at seeing him walk through the door. Stupid nerves. We already agreed we weren't doing this with him.

When he sat down beside me, I looked over at him as if just noticing he'd arrived. "Hey, thanks for coming!"

"No problem." He looked closely at me. "Are you feeling better?"

I ducked my head and covered my face. "Yes, and so embarrassed. I can't thank you enough." I peeked through my fingers at him to find him staring at me with a fond expression. "You kicked Tye's ass for me, then made sure I got home. I'm so mortified I got that drunk." I sucked in a deep breath. "Anyway, thanks for coming, then and now."

Rico smiled and reached up. He tucked a stray piece of hair behind my ear. Pleasant chills ran all across my skin. I caught myself leaning into his touch when it lingered too long and abruptly pulled away.

"Frankly, I don't think I kicked it enough, but you can call on me anytime." His voice had that deep, growly quality again, making a blush spread across my skin.

"Okay, let me round up the girls. I've sort of figured out what route for you to take." I was sending the girls with him that I knew already where they lived. I'd wrangle the ones I didn't know. Worst came to worst, I'd let them crash on my living room floor.

We rounded them all up and as he stuffed two into the cab of his truck, he smiled at me.

"Thank you," I whispered. He saluted me, then ran around the truck.

"Okay," I called. "The rest of you pile in my truck!" I had a big cab with a small backseat, so I managed to get the rest in and buckled, with my sister so close she put her head on my shoulder.

"Thanks, sis," she said in a faint voice. I knew she wasn't long before passing out, so I made all the girls give me their addresses before plugging them into my GPS on my phone.

I managed to get them all home. It helped that two of them were staying with Melody. When it was finally just me, I headed home, suddenly exhausted.

To my surprise, Rico's truck sat in my driveway. He stood resting casually against the passenger door, hands tucked in his pockets. His dark brown hair looked black in the waning moonlight, but his eyes still sparkled.

"Hey." I slid out of my truck and looked at him quizzically.

"I just wanted to make sure you got home okay."

It was so strange how my heart raced at the thought of him coming to check on me. What the hell did I care that he'd cared enough to come to check on me? He walked closer, and my heart nearly beat out of my chest.

"I can hear your heart pounding," he whispered. I barely heard him. All the blood was in the process of rushing straight to my head. Well, some of it had gone directly south. It was torn, really, and it was making me dizzy.

Rico put his hands on both my cheeks and stared into my eyes. "Breathe," he whispered. "You don't have to be nervous. I'd never do anything without your consent."

I consented. Oh, I consented. But my lips wouldn't move to tell him I wanted him to kiss me. Damn, but I wanted him to kiss me silly.

Rico smirked like he knew exactly what I was thinking. Leaning in, he pressed his lips to the corner of my mouth. My skin lit up at the tiny contact, and the rest of the blood went south.

Then he pulled back, leaving me aching for more.

"Goodnight," Rico whispered as his hands fell away from my face.

Oh, hell no. No fucking way. I reached out and snagged his arm, tugging him back to me and cupping his face the way he had mine. Pressing my lips firmly to his, I gave him a real kiss goodnight. His body molded to mine, pressing me against the truck, and his lips parted enough that I slipped one of mine between and sucked his bottom lip into my mouth with a moan.

When Rico returned my moan, and I knew he was just as turned on as I was, I let go of his face. "Goodnight," I whispered with a smirk.

If I was going to spend the night turned on and unsatisfied, so was he.

Chapter 12 - Rico

Having Monday off turned out to be a pain in my ass. I was restless, on edge, and incredibly irritable. All I could think about was Kara. Her lips, her body. How she'd pulled me back to her to give me the world's most amazing goodnight kiss.

My skin crawled all day and half the night until I finally fell asleep. That's how eager I was to get back to work.

I was so worried about how things were going to go. What if it didn't work out? What if she thought it was an enormous mistake? What would I do then?

Oh, damn it. I didn't even care about the inheritance. Not anymore. They could fucking keep it. If I screwed things up with Kara, that would be the real loss.

On Tuesday morning, as I parked my truck in front of the office, I had no idea how I was going to handle this. Should I pretend it never happened? I didn't want it to be awkward.

But miraculously, it wasn't. I walked in the maintenance office and Kara's gaze swung up from her phone. Her face turned as red as a tomato.

Valor growled in satisfaction when her heart raced as soon as she saw me. He was totally self-satisfied.

She'd definitely wanted that kiss and based on the way her heart beat a pattern in her chest, she wanted more. And damn, I wanted to give her more. Nine in the morning and my pants were already protesting.

Valor had finally stopped being so forlorn, mainly because he knew what I hadn't admitted even to myself yet. I had to see where this was going to go with Kara. I couldn't just walk away from her.

Normally, I'd just go in and take what I wanted—provided the woman was willing. I wasn't a monster. But in this case, I couldn't. Kara was different. With her, I felt completely different. I had to let her take the lead. I wouldn't make a move unless she asked.

Surprisingly, I was completely content with that thought, and so was Valor. As long as I was open to the relationship and we'd be spending a lot of time around Kara, he was happy.

Not only was Kara different, but I was. I wanted to make her proud. I wanted to take care of her and prove that I could make a great partner for her.

"How are you feeling?"

She chuckled. "I feel great. I got over my hangover, but my poor sister." She shook her head. "She didn't feel the effects the first night, but after the second I thought she was going to puke all day. She called me early, crying." She chuckled with a slightly evil undertone. "So, I went over and made her an early, loud breakfast."

I didn't quite understand the delight she seemed to have at making breakfast. Must've been a sister thing, but it made me smile to see her happy.

We made small talk for a while and went over our scheduled projects for the week. More would appear through the app or phone calls, too. They always did.

Our first call was quite a drive up the mountain. At first, the atmosphere in the truck was tense. The kiss we'd shared hung in the cab, unspoken and weighing on both of us.

I wouldn't be the one to bring it up. Nope.

With a long, drawn-out sigh, she finally gave in. "So. We kissed," she said bluntly.

I froze and looked at her out of the corner of my eye. "We did."

"You tried to give me a small kiss, but I took it too far," she said, her tone almost apologetic. Well, she wasn't allowed to apologize for that kiss. That was mine, she couldn't take it back now.

"I disagree." I'd said I'd let her take the lead, and I had. She brought it up, after all.

"Yes, I'm attracted to you. But it can't affect my work. I can't just get up and find another job somewhere else. If my business fails here, I'd have to move." Her fingers thrummed on the steering wheel. "I don't have another skillset…" She cut her eyes my way. "Or trust funds to fall back on."

"Ouch." I clutched my chest as if her words had cut deep. "Aimed right for the heart. Don't forget, I have a work goal as well. I have time limits I have to meet for a job. The longer I remain gainfully employed, the more I get out of it."

Damn it, that sounded like I was only working for her for the money. "What I mean is, at first that was my only goal, but, Kara, I need you to know I've been enjoying myself. I don't mind coming to work and not just because I like working with you."

Her demeanor lifted, just a little, but her body language opened up and she shot me a couple of looks of curiosity, maybe even excitement. "Oh?"

"I like working with my hands. I like the sense of accomplishment. I've never had a project or job that I completed through and through like when you have me take the lead. I look forward to taking on a job on my own."

In truth, I felt like I was already capable of taking on some of the less difficult jobs, but she hadn't set me free yet. I didn't mind. I wanted to try one totally alone, sure, but that meant less time with Kara.

"We need to be professional." Her voice sounded less sure.

I grinned and pushed, just a little. "I can still be a capable, professional assistant during business hours while giving you the best sex of your life after hours."

She gulped so loud it made Valor chuckle. Her face flushed red and the speed of her heart rate increased as she gripped the steering wheel tighter.

She wanted it and there was no way she could deny it.

But still. I didn't expect her to agree. I figured I still had weeks of working on her to get her to see it was okay to have a relationship with me and still let me work with her.

"Okay," she said firmly with her chin jutted out into the air.

My jaw dropped. If Valor had been in his scales, his would've as well. Shock reverberated through my body, coming from me *and* him. The cab was quiet for a moment, and I could hear the trees rushing past as we drove. Or maybe that was in my head.

My dick hardened in my work jeans as she spoke, and the knowledge of what was going to happen washed over me. "We can test your theory on Friday night. Come over after work." She glanced at me quickly, then amended her statement. "Uh, at eight."

She probably wanted time to primp. Most girls seemed to. That was fine with me, I'd want to primp a bit of my own.

Shit. Friday. It was only Tuesday morning. How was I going to make it until damn Friday?

The rest of the week, I focused on learning about maintenance, construction, and anything I could get my hands on. I put all my energy into cramming as much knowledge into my head as I could and tried to keep my other head out of it.

It didn't help one fucking bit. The week still crept by like a snail with a bad back. And every assignment we went on together was torture. The only upside was that Kara began letting me take on a few assignments on my own. That helped slightly.

When we worked together, I couldn't stop myself from touching her. I tried to keep it light. I was ever aware that women didn't always like men to be handsy. But Kara didn't seem to mind when I brushed her wrist or put my hand on her shoulder. If I leaned in close to study some repair she'd made, I used the time wisely to bask in her delectable scent.

By the time Friday finally rolled around, I was nearly in a damn frenzy, and Kara's unspoken clues told me she felt the same. Her heartbeat seemed permanently elevated and she'd begun touching me in the same ways I did her. A hand lightly ran across my back as she squeezed past me in a pantry as we repaired shelves. Her hand on my arm when she laughed at one of my jokes.

Small, seemingly insignificant movements that made my dick stand at half-mast *all* the time. My daily showers just weren't cutting it anymore.

It was a glorious ache I couldn't wait to relieve.

The thought of being mated still made me feel uneasy, but I wanted Kara on a primal level that I couldn't deny if I tried.

We finished our last job of the day. Friday's workload was pretty light, thankfully. As we packed up our tools and put them away at the shop, Kara cleared her throat. "I'll see you later?"

"I'm really looking forward to it." I smiled at her and had to remind myself we both needed time to freshen up before this happened. Neither of us would be as comfortable after a half-day of sweating and dirt.

She had a smudge of grease on her cheek that made me smile.

"What?" She shifted her beautiful eyes uncomfortably.

"You're cute."

Her blush was answer enough. "Oh, stop it. I'll see you soon. Lock up for me."

She practically ran from the room. I finished up and turned off the lights. As much as I was looking forward to tonight, something had me on edge.

Driving home, I went slow and dissected my feelings, trying to figure out why I wasn't totally focused on the fun we were about to have.

You're used to more excitement.

Valor's words rang with a resonance of truth. This life, compared to how I used to live, was kind of boring.

I parked in the barn and trudged across the yard, listening for anyone inside. The house was totally silent. It was barely past lunchtime, so nobody expected me anyway.

As I walked up the stairs to my room, I had a moment of missing my old life. The excitement, the adrenaline. It was a head rush every day.

While I waited for the shower water to heat up, I thought about my old contacts. It wouldn't have been too difficult to throw something together really quick. Pull off a quick get-rich-quick scheme on some wealthy woman. Maybe spend some time on a motorcycle, hitting bars all over the states.

Then Kara's face flashed through my mind.

You've got something to lose now.

Mated or not mated, the last thing I wanted to do was let Kara down. Even if I managed to disappear for a week without my family suspecting, Kara would know something wasn't right.

Guilt plagued me for even considering going back to my old ways.

You're growing.

He was right again. A couple of months ago, I would've been gone before the plans were fully formed in my mind.

Hey. At least I was heading in the right direction, right?

I finished getting ready with a smile on my face. Shaving wasn't as easy with a grin plastered to my lips, but I managed it with only one nick under my chin.

After the longest week of my life, it was finally showtime. I popped a strand of condoms in my pocket, adjusted my pants, and jaunted down the stairs to go find my mate.

***

Back and forth. Back and forth. Back, pause, and forth again.

The grin still on my face, I waited and listened to her being nervous as my hand remained poised to knock on Kara's door, as it had been for the last five minutes. The anticipation was killing her, as it might've been me if I hadn't found myself amused by her pacing when I arrived. What would she think when she saw the care I'd put into my appearance tonight? Was the rose too much?

Shaking my head, I finally let my hand fall in three quick raps. Kara's footsteps stopped suddenly, then slowly approached the door. When it opened, I made sure to hold the rose out so that it was the first thing she saw. She gasped in surprise, an utterly delectable sound, her soft lips forming a perfect O as she plucked the rose from my fingers.

I took her in as she smiled, her eyes closed, nose buried in the fragrant flower. She was wearing—dear God—shorts. Small denim shorts and a green tank top that highlighted her eyes and made them glow. Her feet were bare, with dark pink toenails, and her golden-brown hair had been released from its usual ponytail, tumbling in loose waves that I longed to bury my hands in. The casual combo brought out her feminine beauty better than any expensive designer clothes could have.

Mine.

Valor surged us forward, and I went with him willingly, kicking the door shut behind me as my lips crashed into Kara's, and I tangled my fingers in her silky locks. The sound of her shock was muffled, almost instantly replaced by a groan of desire that stoked a fire in my core. I backed her against the wall and grabbed her thighs, lifting her easily as she wrapped herself around me, lips never leaving mine. I managed to elicit another groan from her as I pressed my rapidly growing desire into her center. The rose fell to the floor beside us.

In the back of my mind, I vaguely registered the smell of food, but my stomach was not currently the one in control at the moment. Gripping her tightly, I navigated us to her bedroom, a task made only slightly more difficult by the fact that we were seemingly starved for each other, unable to pull away even for breath. When my legs met the edge of the mattress, I lowered her to the pillow-covered bed, running my palm across her bare thighs, over the tight shorts, and gently brushing my fingertips across her stomach where her tank top had ridden up.

I pulled away just enough to meet her eyes questioningly. Kara bit her lip nervously but nodded and started wriggling away to pull her shirt off. I grabbed her arms, stopping her and shaking my head. Oh, no, there was no way I was going to rush this. I traced my nose along her cheek and down along the column of her throat, inhaling the scent of her, sending a shudder of pleasure through her. Placing gentle kisses, I worked my way down, making sure to mark every bit of skin the shirt left exposed.

Her emerald eyes watched, curious, expectant, hesitant, as I lifted the shirt and kissed a path down to her belly button, then delved my tongue inside it. A tiny whimper escaped her, but that was all I needed. Her shirt rolled up further and she grabbed the edges and chucked it across the room, moaning loudly as my mouth latched onto one of her nipples. Her breathing was already starting to puff out more erratically, and I'd only just gotten started. Valor and I wanted to push her to the brink over and over again until she forgot her own name.

We'd make sure she remembered mine.

As my tongue swirled over the nub, my hand freed the button on her shorts. I felt her fingers brush across my temple, then dive into my hair and grab on as she arched into me, gasping. I switched sides, giving equal attention to each breast, and slipped my hand into her shorts. Damn, she was so wet already! She whimpered again, thrusting herself eagerly against my fingers. It was testing my restraint painfully, but I was determined to make good on my word.

I pulled my hand free and released her nipple, nice and hard now after my attention, and kissed my way down her stomach again, my tongue flicking out over her skin after each kiss. She gasped and writhed, pulling at my hair urgently. I grasped the waistband of her shorts, catching her eyes again for permission. She pulled herself onto her elbows and nodded, her face flushed. I grinned; I had done that to her. Well, if she liked that little bit, she was in for a hell of a surprise.

Slowly, I tugged the denim and the little green panties off until they dropped unceremoniously to the floor. Her intoxicating scent made my head swim pleasantly. I sank to the floor, pulling at her legs until her ass rested on the edge of the bed. She continued to watch me, her pupils dilated, as I licked and nipped at her inner thighs, wrapping my arms around them to hold her in place. Just when I started to close in on her sex, I moved to the other thigh. She groaned, throwing her head back in frustration, and I kept grinning as I administered my affection across her toned legs.

Just as her head lifted again to watch, I plunged my tongue inside her. She dropped back and pushed against my mouth, her breath catching in her throat. I found she tasted so much sweeter than I had even anticipated, and a rumbling growl ripped its way out of my mouth, the vibration on her most sensitive areas causing her to convulse and whimper. Her fingers tightened almost painfully on my scalp as my tongue swirled around the sensitive nub before tracing back to her opening. She was the only food I was craving, and I intended to eat my fill.

Focusing on her swollen clit, I carefully inserted a finger below it, slipping it in with no resistance whatsoever. That was interesting. I thrust a few times and she bucked back, then I added another. Her hands left my hair and she grabbed a pillow, pressing it to her face to muffle her cries. I stood, my fingers still thrusting, and snatched the pillow away, tossing it across the room. She looked up at me, confusion and ecstasy warring across her face.

"I want to hear every sound you can make," I told her, my voice husky with need.

She could only nod as I settled back down between her legs, putting my tongue and lips to work, licking and sucking until she couldn't take a proper breath. I twisted my wrist and curled my fingers inside her, causing her to cry out as I hit her sensitive spot. When she reached for my hair again, I grabbed her wrist with my free hand and guided it to her own breast. She took the hint and started massaging them, rubbing the pads of her thumbs over her nipples. Holy shit, that was so hot. I strained against my pants, but I needed to push her over the edge first.

Pumping faster, curling my fingers at the peak of every thrust, I sucked hard on her clit, my tongue flicking over the tip. Kara cried out and arched her back off the bed, tightening hard around my fingers even as her channel flooded with her arousal.

"—co, ohmigod, Rico," she gasped, reaching for me. "Now, please."

I wiped at my mouth and let her sit up, where she instantly tugged at my shirt. My belt hit the floor near her shirt, and after I snagged a condom from my pocket, my pants followed. She stared hungrily at my manhood, precum already glistening at the tip. Gulping hard, she reached for it, mouth quickly swallowing it before I could object. Hard as I was, I almost came instantly and had to grab her shoulders to ease her back. She frowned at me.

"I wanted to return the favor," she explained, looking nervous now.

"No," I replied gently. "Tonight, I'm the boss, and I want you to lie back."

A wicked grin crossed her face as she did what I said. I ripped the package open with my teeth and knelt back down between her legs and, giving a few more licks to stoke her heat back up as I rolled the condom on, slid my fingers in again. Still swollen and sensitive from the first one, I pumped and sucked and licked until she came hard again.

She gasped for breath as I continued, grabbing my cock with my free hand and giving a good squeeze. Her taste was overwhelming, and I was so hard that there probably wasn't any blood left in my head to think straight. My fingers and tongue stroked and pushed her through a third orgasm and then she pulled away.

I grabbed her left leg as I stood and positioned myself at her entrance, setting her foot on my shoulder and kissing her toes. I grabbed my length, running it across her slit and coating it in her juices, then carefully started easing into her. I pressed my forehead into her foot, squeezing my eyes closed in concentration, trying my damnedest not to just slam into her viciously until she screamed my name loud enough for the neighbors to hear.

Kara wrapped her other leg around me and pulled hard, sliding me home, and I almost fell over at the intensity, the unequivocal rightness of it. Her green eyes met my hazel ones, and for a moment, the world froze. She felt it too; she had to.

Slowly, I pulled my hips back and thrust again, keeping a hold on her leg, kissing her adorable ankle. She opened her mouth, but no noise came out, and her pupils were blown out. I drove into her again, slowly but surely picking up a rhythm, making sure I wouldn't end it too soon. After the week of anticipation, this was driving me nuts.

"Harder," she whispered, one hand tangling in her hair as the other one teased her breast again. "Please."

That was all the encouragement I needed. Who was I to deny her? I adjusted my angle, bracing one hand on the bed, and increased my pace, ramming into her ruthlessly to the rhythm of her cries. I felt myself stiffening too soon and paused, pulling out and flipping her over on the bed, pulling her ass up and slamming into her again. Every noise she made was music to my ears, and I could practically hear Valor's need pressing against my skull.

Gripping her hip with one hand, I leaned forward against her backside to reach around and slide my fingers between her slick folds. She bucked back against me, finding her own rhythm, and she tightened around me. I was gonna lose it too soon. I didn't want to be anywhere near done with her yet, but I found I didn't even care as long as she came with me. My fingers continued their ministrations as my groin slapped noisily against her cheeks, and far too soon, fireworks exploded behind my eyes.

"Ric— ah!" she screamed as she followed me over the edge.

A few more thrusts as I came hard, and I had to lean over on her, pressing my forehead into her spine and gasping for breath. Holy shit, that was… not what I was expecting at all. I noted that Valor had retreated, purring contentedly like some huge, scaly cat. Whatever doubts I'd had earlier about mating with this woman didn't seem to exist at this moment, both of us sweaty and spent. This feeling might be something I could see myself getting used to.

She was dangerous.

Chapter 13 - Kara

Rico's face buried in my neck made me want to flip over and start it all again. But I doubted even he could rev up and go again this fast. I mean… probably?

His heavy breaths puffed down my neck toward my chest, puckering my nipples. But still, he didn't move. His breathing was heavy but somehow didn't sound like it should have if it was just exertion.

"Are you okay?" I craned my neck to see him, and his face didn't look tired. He looked like he was in pain. He kept his eyes closed as his breathing calmed down.

When he spoke back to me, it was through gritted teeth. "Just riding it out," he said. "Do you ever feel like you've got a beast inside you that you've just got to control?"

I burst out laughing. "No, not at all."

He finally opened his eyes and pulled himself out of me with a groan. "So, good. It's just me then." He took care of the condom as I rolled over on the bed and wiggled up to rest on the pillows.

"Listen." Rico stood, stark naked, his dick still mostly hard—wow!—and put his hands on his hips. "We've got to talk about all these pillows."

I snuggled deeper in my pile of fluff and smiled contentedly. "We most certainly do not have to talk about my pillows. I love my pillows and you can hush."

Rico launched himself at me, landing half on top of me and half on the pile of pillows. "If we make this a regular exercise, and I hope we do, I'm going to need more room on this bed. These things take up half of it."

I turned on my side and smiled at him. I would've expected to be embarrassed about being naked and on my side. Even my small breasts looked weird from this angle. But Rico looked at me with a smile in his eyes. Sort of an admiration. I found I couldn't bring myself to be self-conscious around him.

That was a nice surprise. I guessed that was what the best sex of my life got me. Inhibition.

"I'll show you my inner beast sometime," Rico said as he scooted closer to me. "He's not as scary as you'd think."

I giggled, going along with the joke. "Oh, I'd love to see him, especially if he makes you do more of that."

Rico puffed out a gust of air. "Shit. That was nothing. I held back as long as I could and gave as much foreplay as I could stand, but it being our first time together, it went far faster than I wanted it to. You are just… Damn. I promise, we'll build up to some real doozies."

I glowed under his words. I'd never had anything close to as good as what he'd just given me, much less a *doozy.*

Damn, but I was game to give it a try. My blood was already warming up for another round and I had to fight it back, give Rico a chance to come down. Regardless of how porn made it look, I knew real men couldn't keep that up indefinitely, no matter how in shape he was. I was certainly willing to put him to the test, though, in time.

We snuggled and talked for a long time until I remembered the dinner I'd left sitting on the stove. Luckily, it had finished cooking, so nothing would be burning, but it would all be cold. "Shoot," I whispered. "Dinner."

Rico's eyes lit up. "I'm starving."

I rolled off the bed and picked up my discarded clothes, untangling them and dressing as I talked. "I didn't have time to do much, not that I'm that great of a cook anyway. It's just some baked chicken and veggies."

"I love baked chicken and veggies," he said. "If you know how to season, that is."

I blanched and looked at him. He was already mostly dressed.

Too bad. I could've gotten really used to him walking around in the buff, or close to it. He was freaking hot. "My father, well, foster father, says I tend to overseason."

Rico grinned and pulled his shirt down over his head. "Good. My kind of seasoning."

After I popped our plates in the microwave to reheat them, we sat at the table to eat. Conversation flowed much easier than I expected it to.

"You've mentioned having a foster father once or twice since I've known you," Rico said. "And you told me a bit about your parents that drunk night."

I rolled my eyes. "Yeah, sorry. I'm not sure what all I told you, but I'm not secretive with it or anything." I gave him a quick rundown again. "My biological parents were crackheads. They live here in town and have no idea who I am. I changed my name to my foster family's name. By the time I found them, I was a bit old for adoption, so I just changed my name. I love them very much, and Melody feels like a real sister to me, but somehow, I never could get to calling him Dad. I guess I was too old when we met."

"Do you consider him your father?" Rico asked.

I nodded, smiling at the idea. "I do. If I ever get married, he'll be the one to walk me down the aisle. I call him for advice and stuff. He worries about me until I hire practically useless apprentices." I winked at him to let him know I wasn't serious about him being useless. "I help him work on old cars when I get time. He's my dad."

He chuckled. "Ah, so he's the one I have to thank for a job. Hopefully soon I'll carry my own weight."

Shrugging, I scooped up another bite. "He heard about the incident with Nick through the local gossip channels. Wanted me to be safe and hire some help." I flashed him a smile. "And you're doing a great job. You'll be flying circles around me in no time."

Rico gave me a sharp look, but then relaxed and smiled. His eyes lowered to his plate. "I get it. My Uncle Perry and grandparents raised me after my parents died."

I couldn't help my wide eyes. I hadn't known his parents had died. He'd carefully avoided discussing them in previous conversations, but I hadn't thought much of it since it wasn't such a great topic for me, either. Now it made more sense.

"You grew up without parents, too?" I asked.

He sighed and nibbled on the vegetables. He'd eaten three servings of chicken but barely touched his veggies. Like a dang kid. But it was cute.

"Yeah, a car accident. My uncle mostly raised me. My grandfather is the head of a large family business and it keeps him very busy. I guess they spoiled me a bit, and it took me longer than I would've liked to realize I'd become someone I didn't want to be."

He couldn't meet my eyes.

"You know, I think it's okay for someone like us, who went through something that traumatic, especially you losing your parents like that… Well, I think it's okay if it takes us a bit longer in life to figure out where we fit in and what course we want to be on." I reached out and touched his hand. "I'm sure your family understands that, too."

"They do." He squeezed my fingers and didn't let go. "I think they're making me work now to try to undo some of the damage they inflicted by letting me get away with murder for so long." He chuckled wryly. "I should give them more shit along the way, really."

His words sounded like a spoiled kid, but his tone proved he was very fond of them and appreciated their efforts. I remembered how he'd talked about his aunt making sure he was well fed at home. I recognized the signs, now, of a caring family trying to help someone cope with loss. I ran my thumb lightly across his fingers.

"Cut them some slack, too. They lost family, too, right?"

He nodded. "Yeah. They did."

I sighed, thinking about what he had. "Hey, think about the good things. You could've been a part of a small family and ended up in the system. At least you had an uncle and grandparents to raise you, right?" I didn't mean to sound jealous, but a hint of the green monster must've been in my voice because Rico squeezed my hand again.

"You're absolutely right. I'm sorry you didn't have that."

The conversation lagged for a few minutes until Rico sat back and patted his belly. It did look slightly rounder than it had before. "So now what?" he asked. "I'm going to be honest with you, I don't want to leave, but we said we'd keep things as professional as we could."

I looked from him to my bedroom door. If at all possible, I wanted another taste of what he gave me before.

"I mean…" I grinned at him and slipped the shoulder of my tank top off. "These aren't technically business hours, right?"

I couldn't help but squeal when he growled and launched himself around the table at me. I ran for my bedroom on my tiptoes, and he caught me as I went through the door.

Time for round two.

Chapter 14 - Rico

My first six weeks were passing by like a speeding freight train. Nearly a week after Kara and I had sex at her house, we found ourselves finally replacing the part on the air conditioner at the gym. It had taken it that long just to come in.

Kara, without any explanation, had stopped assigning me jobs to do on my own, and we did everything together. I didn't complain once. She had me take the lead as often as possible, standing in the background and occasionally giving advice.

Not today, of course. "This is a complicated repair," she said. "On top of that, it is a matter of pride that I am the one to handle everything at the gym. I can't let them think that because I hired a man, suddenly they don't have to deal with me anymore."

I chuckled and patted her hand on the seat beside me in her truck. "You can take the lead as often as you'd like." I turned the statement into an innuendo by curling up my lip and wagging my eyebrows at her.

She burst out laughing, throwing her head back. "Yeah, see, you say that now, but when I get you in the sack, you always take control."

She was right, but I couldn't help that. I was an alpha, as was Valor, of course. It was hard enough that I was able to give up control in the workplace, and something I was quite proud of, actually. I would be more than willing to try letting her dominate in the bedroom, I just wasn't sure how well it would go. "Maybe we could give it a shot, with the understanding that it might not work."

She giggled, and even though we'd had sex every night since the first time last Friday, at her house, at the office, and in the cab of her truck, still, she blushed. Damn, she was cute.

"Let's get this over with." I carried the tool bag and she grabbed the part and we didn't even check in at the front desk. There was no need—we knew what needed to be done, and we just wanted to get the job finished and over with.

Kara was right, as she usually was. It was a very complicated job, but I watched closely and to my delight, I was able to keep up and understand everything that she did. If it happened again, I was confident I would be able to replace a part like this on my own.

As I watched Kara work, Valor preened. She had a glow about her that had started Friday night. There was a spring in her step and a sparkle in her eyes. I knew I'd put that there. And I wasn't the only one who had noticed. Men seemed to be drawn to Kara more than before. Maybe it was just my jealousy noticing it now that we were connected.

Even though the repair went pretty straightforward, it still took almost an hour to install. The sun beat down on us, and my shirt was starting to stick to my back. By the time we finished up, I looked like I'd been working out alongside the other muscle heads inside, and the gym had filled up with the morning crowd.

Usually, this time of the morning was filled with moms who dropped the kids off at school and then came for a workout. But today, as soon as we walked out of the stairway and into the gym proper, I spotted him at the front desk. The asshole from the bar.

He glared at me but didn't engage me. Oh, no. The guy was a total dick and a coward. Instead, he directed his words to Kara. "Dragging your bodyguard along with you? In case you tease a man and then try to leave him high and dry again?"

Fuck, no. I stepped forward and set the bag of tools down a little too hard, ready to tear his fucking head off. The kid behind the counter hurriedly moved to the other side and tried to look busy. Tye's smirk faltered as I approached.

Teach him a lesson.

Valor's anger was so intense I nearly growled at the dickhead. The only thing that stopped me was Kara jumping in front of me and putting her hand on my chest.

I looked down into her endless green gaze, and I knew I'd do whatever she wanted me to. So would Valor.

"Please," she whispered. The one word was all it took. I still wanted to rip his head from his shoulders, but I was able to stop myself.

She tossed her ponytail haughtily behind her and glared at Tye. "I know that's not how it happened and so do you. Kid yourself all you want to, but you're a pervert, and if I'm right, a rapist, ever since high school. Maybe that's the only way you can get fucked, by tricking or forcing a woman."

She sniffed and walked away from him.

Tye glared at her. When he opened his mouth to retort, Valor's growl ripped from my chest. Tye snapped his jaw shut and looked at me in surprise. "Stay away from her," I said in a voice quiet enough that she wouldn't hear it.

He swallowed audibly. The sound of his heart beating a rapid pace filled my ears. He was terrified of me but would probably never show it.

With one last step toward him, I grabbed the tools and followed Kara back out the door, loading our stuff into the truck.

"Come on," she sighed. "Let's go get lunch."

We'd begun to enjoy getting lunch from the diner or grocery store and sitting on the back of her truck under a copse of trees in the parking lot of the local park. Usually, enough of a breeze would kick up to keep us pretty cool as we ate and talked. And sometimes made out.

"I haven't asked," I said after we finished eating. "I didn't want to pry. But what is your history with that guy?"

Kara sighed and kicked her feet back and forth over the edge of the tailgate. "After you kicked his ass, I thought about telling you, but it's so embarrassing. I hated to do it."

I doubted there was anything she could tell me that would make me like her less. "Hey," I said gently.

"Come on. It's me. I think we're friends enough by now that you can talk to me, right?"

She ducked her head and nodded. "Yeah, I just hate it." I kept my hand on her thigh as she continued. "In high school, I was small, and I didn't hit puberty until I was almost seventeen. And even then…" She sat up and indicated her small breasts.

"Hey," I protested. "I love them!"

She giggled and put her hand on mine but wouldn't look at me. "Tye was the popular guy. Quarterback, valedictorian, rich family, the whole package. Every girl had a crush on him. And I was the shy, quiet girl, always hiding in the back of the class, always wearing all black."

Suspicions of what was coming with the story began to grow in my gut. I had a sneaking suspicion I knew what had happened and it made my stomach queasy.

"They—his football buddies—made a bet that Tye could get into my pants, and I was stupid and gullible, and it worked. The next day, my panties were hanging from the flagpole, and Tye…"

She brushed tears away as I tried not to tighten my fingers around her leg. I didn't want to hurt her, but I was so angry I didn't know if I could contain myself.

You must agree that we have to hurt him.

If only it was that easy. "I should've killed him when I had the chance." They were my words but in Valor's voice. We were in accord for once, and if Tye had been standing in front of us, we wouldn't have been able to stop ourselves.

My stomach churned as she continued her story. "Cynthia was almost as bad as Tye afterward. She wanted him, and she basically was the female version of him. Captain of the cheerleading squad and all that. She wasn't smart like Tye, though, and he couldn't stand her. That was one thing he'd told me when he was working on me that I think was true. He'd liked our conversations because they were intelligent."

The look of disgust on her face made me even angrier. She wasn't just hurt by this, even all these years later. She was ashamed, grossed out.

"What he did," I said in a low voice, "that was rape."

She shook her head. "I was willing, at the time."

"No!" I jumped to the ground and took her hands, tapping her chin so she'd look at me. "He got you to sleep with him under false pretenses. In my book, that's rape. I'm so sorry."

I wrapped my arms around her and held her close, wishing with all my heart I had the sort of magic that would let me go back in time and change this for her. She had so much pain and carried it so close to her all the time. My problems seemed laughable compared to what she'd been through.

"You're squishing me," Kara whispered.

I channeled my rage deep inside, curled in a ball to work off later, and forced myself to chuckle and loosen my grip. "Come on. We've still got a few places to hit before we're done."

She sighed and hopped off the tailgate. "Yep."

After a moment's hesitation, she held out the keys to her precious truck. "Wanna drive?"

My jaw dropped and I restrained myself from snatching the keys away in my excitement. "Have you ever let anyone drive your truck?"

Kara's beautiful green eyes squinted as she considered my question. "Just my dad."

"Then hell yes!" I exclaimed. The horror at the story she'd told me sat heavy in my gut. I knew I'd have to deal with it somehow or else hunt Tye down and teach him another lesson.

But for Kara's sake, I kept the rest of the day light. I pretended to have a hard time driving the truck, made jokes, and generally made myself a spirit-lifter. I made her laugh several times, which was a definite improvement.

Now I knew why she hated snobs so much. And I was so glad I'd changed and was continuing to change so that I could be someone that would never remind her of those sorts of people again.

For the first time since our first time, we weren't spending the night together. Her sister had asked her to go shopping with her, then to a late dinner.

Back at the shop, I kissed her plump lips several times. "I find I don't want to separate, knowing we aren't meeting up later," I whispered.

She dropped her forehead to my chest. "Me too! And that's crazy, because we've been together pretty much nonstop. But Melody will probably want to spend the night. I'll see you in the morning. Nine, sharp."

With one last kiss, I said goodbye. "Nine."

As soon as she drove a way, I texted the guys. I needed advice. Pronto.

It turned out that Charlotte, my cousin Axel's wife, had a late shift at the hospital in the next town over, where she was a nurse. Their son, Chase, was spending the night with his grandma—which meant he'd be at the manor.

Having dinner at Axel's was perfect. I headed straight to the manor for a fast shower, using the outside bathroom instead of going in and having to explain my absence to Aunt Carla and Uncle James. Not that they would mind, but a conversation with them could drag out longer than I had time for.

After tying clothes into a bag and wrapping it around my neck loosely, I let Valor take the lead and fly us to Axel's huge cabin way up in the woods. It was on Kingston land, so there was no danger of flying over a road or house where we could be spotted. This land was patrolled constantly, not only by Kingstons but by the local wolf pack, who used the land for their shifts as well. They were much more plentiful than the dragons and patrolled in shifts in exchange for a safe place to shift. It was a great symbiotic relationship.

Once Valor had his head, he wanted to go find Tye. I had to remind him of the consequences of a dragon flying over Black Claw and searching out a human to kill. He didn't care, but I sure as hell did.

By the time I convinced him to quit dawdling and go to Axel's, everyone else was already there. Valor landed in the back yard as the daylight began to wane to twilight. They waved, making no mention to my nakedness, as was our way. After I dressed, I jogged over to the porch and accepted the beer Maddox held out.

"Thanks for coming," I said. Looking around the porch, I realized the entire clan was here. Every dragon, even my Uncle James.

"Son, we're here for you," he said, clapping me on the back.

"That's right," our alpha, Maverick, chimed in. "You're a Kingston. And while you're staying in Black Claw, you're just as much a part of our local pack as my own son."

Maddox gulped his beer and nodded. "True."

Jury and Stefan sat around Axel's big table and watched. The smiles on their faces showed their agreement.

"Sit," Axel said. "I had just enough time to swing by the grocery store for steaks on the way home, and they're done unless you want them cooked well done."

Everyone protested and rushed to sit around the table.

"Start talking," Maverick said as Axel passed food around. I looked down at my steak, cooked perfectly to the way I liked it, and said a quick thanks.

I didn't have my parents, but I still had family who accepted me, even after I'd been such a dick. Hopefully I was changing that.

"It's Kara. And Valor," I said.

Maddox wagged his eyebrows at me. "Took you long enough."

They all laughed and elbowed each other.

"No," I protested. "I mean, yes, but there's a problem." I paused. "Well, two. Let me tell you the newest one. There's a guy in town that's a problem." I described Tye and gave a vague recounting of what he'd done to Kara. I didn't want to tell her secret, but the guy had to be dealt with. Maybe Maverick and Uncle James, the police chief, could figure it out.

I was right. When I finished telling them all I could, James and Maverick exchanged a glance. "We'll look into it and see what we can do the legal way rather than vigilante justice."

A few months ago, vigilante justice would've been my only choice. I wouldn't have even told them about it. While I knew going the legal, human way was the right thing to do, it didn't feel good.

I wanted to kill him.

"Okay, so Kara and I have been spending a lot of time together," I explained. They all laughed and elbowed each other again, so I had to hold my hands up. "Calm down. It's great, of course, but there's a problem."

"They make a pill for that," Jury said around a big wad of steak.

The rest of us laughed, even me. It was a good burn. "I know, I saw them in your cabinet," I retorted. When everyone calmed down their laughter, I continued. "But this is serious. More than once, when emotions have been heated, Valor has been able to speak through me. My voice changes to something else, something that I recognize as Valor. I can usually curb him back quickly, but I can't stop it happening."

"Until you bite her, he'll be able to do that," Maverick said. "I've heard of this as a side effect when a dragon is really set on a mate."

"Well, when we're together..." I shifted uncomfortably. I wasn't one for 'locker room talk'. "You know, intimately, it's all I can do to stop Valor from claiming her. We almost shifted a few times, and last night was the worst. I was so relieved when she said she had plans with her sister tonight. I didn't know what to do."

"I've never had Artemis try to speak through me," Maddox said. We looked around the table, but everyone shook their heads.

"Eros says it's possible," Stefan said. "But usually only when a dragon is a strong alpha."

I am the strongest.

I chuckled and repeated Valor's words.

"That explains it," Maverick said. He chuckled. "Zephyr says he could do it if he wanted to." He leaned forward and whispered. "I think he's jealous that he's never tried."

"You're going to have to negotiate with Valor until you feel Kara is ready for the truth," James said. "Keep him leashed."

Valor growled at that. He didn't like the idea of being forced to do anything he didn't agree to.

It wasn't just Kara, though. I had to be ready. I still wasn't at all sure I would be staying in Black Claw. I still wanted to go far away. Sure, I was having a nice time here, but would I want to be here forever?

As the sun set around us, and my family talked and joked and laughed, I realized something. The thought of staying wasn't as bad as it once was. But still, I couldn't show Valor to Kara until I knew I was ready. Until I wanted to take her as a real mate. With the bond and all that came along with it.

Even thinking it was possible spoke volumes. I was changing. I just had to decide how much I wanted to change.

Chapter 15 - Kara

Every time I thought about Rico coming over for dinner that night, butterflies invaded my stomach. I wasn't even entirely sure what was in my shopping cart at this point, just that I probably needed it. At least I was fairly certain I was sticking to my list, except for this random box of Cheez-Ups that mysteriously appeared and went on the conveyor with the rest because, hey, why not?

These last few days with him had been nice, and I was coming to find that I really liked the person I was getting to know. He was nothing like what I had originally thought, that arrogant, self-absorbed guy he pretended to be. I'd lifted the mask and seen the noble heart behind it, and I hoped it would stick around.

Before I'd even made it to the parking lot, something began to bother me. A sense that I couldn't explain made me anxious and on edge. Women's intuition, I'd always called it. Quickly, I hurried to my truck and loaded the groceries as fast as I could. The hair on the back of my neck prickled, and I threw a subtle glance around as I loaded my bags. I didn't see anything obvious, but it felt like someone was watching me. Maybe it was just my anxiety about the idea of getting serious with someone. Yeah, that might be it.

Maybe not, too. I had pepper spray in my purse, but it was in the truck. I hated carrying a handbag and usually left it under the passenger seat. A whole lot of good it was going to do me in there if I got attacked out here.

I dumped the cart off in the corral and skittered back to my truck, checking all of my mirrors for pursuit as I drove off. The feeling followed me all the way home, even if my invisible stalker didn't, and I was nearing a panic attack by the time I got the shopping bags inside. Once the door closed and locked behind me, it dissipated, leaving only a hint of lingering tension in my shoulders.

After a quick shower to wash the feeling away, I cooked on autopilot. The smells didn't quite reach me, my mind back in that parking lot. That was more than just anxiety, I knew, but who in the world would it have been? Someone I knew? A creepy stalker waiting to kidnap me? That sent a chill down my spine. Tye came to mind, of course, but we'd lived in the same town since high school. I'd never run into him in all that time until recently. Surely, he wasn't so upset about it that he'd watch me. But there wasn't anyone else it could've been.

It had to have been mostly in my head.

I was still on edge when Rico arrived. I was happy—relieved, even—to see him, but even I could tell my smile was strained. It wobbled at the edges as if it wasn't sure it was supposed to be on my face.

He glanced around the apartment suspiciously as soon as I let him in. "Is everything okay?"

"Yeah, fine," I answered a little too quickly, cursing myself.

Rico took my hands, my trembling fingers, and met my eyes. "Something is bothering you. Whatever it is, you can tell me. What happened?"

I took in a shaky breath and nodded. "It's so stupid, but it… felt like someone was watching me earlier."

"Here?" he asked, moving to the windows. An air of competence grew around him as if he could take care of any threat with ease. And somehow, I believed he could. I vaguely remember telling him once, in a drunken stupor, that he had predator eyes. It wasn't just in his eyes, though; it was all of him, and it made me feel safe.

"No, no, at the grocery store, in the parking lot. I just—you know those scary stories where the hair stands up on the back of your neck when you're being watched by something? It felt like that. As I said, it's stupid—" I tried to downplay how much it had freaked me out.

"Always trust your instincts, Kara," he said, stepping back toward me and cradling my face in his hands. "We have instincts for a reason. Listen to them."

I nodded, feeling better that he believed me. It was time to move forward and forget this drama, so I gave him my best smile and pulled him toward the table. "I hope you're hungry."

"Always," he answered with a suggestive glint in his eyes. He took a seat, glanced around the kitchen, then asked, "Do you own a gun?"

Frowning, I answered. "What? No, why would I?"

He shrugged and scooped a bite of food in his mouth, chewing not nearly enough before he swallowed. "Would you object to me taking you to a shooting range sometime? Maybe get you certified, find something to keep around here to protect yourself better."

"No, thanks." The food wasn't as good as I'd hoped, and I wondered what step I'd missed while I'd zoned out. "I'm not exactly big on guns. They're too loud, too many different types of bullets to keep up with, and way too easy to accidentally kill someone with."

"Okay, stun gun it is, then," he replied easily with no hint of judgment. "That's fine. Maybe one day we can go shoot for sport." He shrugged as if it was no big deal. "It could be fun."

I laughed, finally feeling the tension dissolve knowing that someone was there for me and had my back if I needed it. "That sounds okay. As long as you don't want me to carry a gun all the time."

"Nah, stun guns are effective enough for a single woman alone. It's not like you live in a particularly dangerous town." He chuckled. "You should see some of the places I've lived."

The conversation shifted into small talk, which seemed to come easily for us, but as we ate, it somehow diverged into our childhoods. We'd talked a little about our families, but nothing in detail. My good mood soured as all the bruises, the smells, the yelling, all came rushing back with one word.

Rico broached the subject. "So, how much do you remember about your parents?"

I glared down at my plate, pushing my food around with my fork. "Enough that I never touched alcohol until pretty recently."

Rico watched me across the table. I could feel his intense gaze on the top of my head. "They… weren't great drunks, then?"

I laughed sardonically. "'Alcoholics' is the term most people use, and yeah, they were the worst kind. They were usually into worse stuff than alcohol, though, and when they combined the two?" I shuddered just thinking about it.

He grimaced, and for a second I thought I saw a flash of red in his eyes. "You said you see them from time to time. Are they still here in Black Claw?"

Looking up, I realized his hazel eyes seemed sad. "Far as I know, yeah. They were, ah, abusive, and deemed unfit to care for me, or so it says on my file. I jumped between homes until I was sixteen, and you know most of what happened after that."

He nodded and took another bite, chewing thoughtfully. "So, if you don't mind my asking, how did you end up so drunk at your sister's birthday thing?"

"Completely unintentional," I replied, grimacing. "I may have lost track of how many shots I'd had, and as I said, I only started recently and don't do it often, so I don't have much tolerance for it. I was always afraid I'd have the same penchant for addiction that my parents had, you know. And after my childhood, abandonment issues were another problem I had to deal with, and I always kind of associated one with the other, so…"

I trailed off, unable to continue that train of thought. Shoveling another bite into my mouth, I'd hoped to avoid answering another question, or at least put it off for precious seconds, but he remained quiet; the only sounds were our forks on the plates. He seemed introspective, and I thought maybe he was getting ready to shut down on me. Had I shared too much? Did he feel sorry for the poor little abused foster kid now? I didn't need anyone's pity, and I decided to tell him so.

Before I could get the words out of my mouth, he stood and walked around the table, kneeling at my side. He took my hand, turning it over in his, smoothing his thumbs across the lines in my palm. When the silence continued, I closed my hand on his fingers, getting his attention. He sighed and finally met my eyes, a pained look on his face.

"I'll, uh," he started uncertainly. "I hate that you ever felt like anyone didn't want you. If I can help it, I don't want you to ever feel that way again."

He pushed up enough to meet my lips with his, a sweet, simple promise. My mind went blank at the tenderness of it. I was in new territory here. Given my previous relationship experience, of which I had laughably little, these were entirely uncharted waters.

Though normally my anxiety would've kicked up at the thought of a solid, stable relationship, someone else to love and leave me, I was pleasantly surprised to find that I wanted it. I wanted this, whatever it was.

"I haven't been the best since my parents died," he said as he rose to his feet, pulling me with him, "but I'm trying to make some changes to my life, and I hope you'll be patient with me while I get things figured out."

I had no idea what he was going on about, though he sounded so sincere. Sure, I'd thought he was arrogant and full of himself when we met, but I hadn't seen any indication that he was a bad guy. What kind of changes did he plan to make? Whatever it was, I trusted him. That thought should've terrified me, but it didn't, and I smiled at him.

My hand traced his jawline, though I couldn't recall telling it to. "I can be as patient as you need."

Rico dipped his head and kissed me, this time firmer, longer. I parted my lips and his tongue wasted no time acquainting itself with mine. I could feel his fingers in my hair again, tugging gently, and it sent a jolt of excitement through my core. He grinned against my lips as if he could sense it, and pulled back, though the tip of his nose still touched mine.

"I don't know," he mused, playfulness dancing in his hazel eyes. "I think we should test that."

"Test wha—ah!" I shrieked as he tossed me over his shoulder.

I might've smacked at him if I hadn't been laughing so hard, but no one had ever manhandled me like that before. In seconds, I was bouncing across my bed, and my face was flushed. It certainly felt hot, but I couldn't pin down why. Rico crawled on the bed toward me, flinging my precious pillows away, and I scooted back until I met the headboard. He put one knee between my legs as he loomed over me.

"We didn't finish eating," I whispered, hoping I looked even an ounce as hot as he did.

"Oh, I still intend to eat," he replied, lifting one dark eyebrow. "I'm just taking my dessert now."

"Ugh, call the cheese factory, I think they're missing a shipment," I laughed. That made his grin widen further.

He sealed his mouth over mine, and I didn't even care how cheesy his line was as long as he kept kissing me like that. My shirt went up over my head, the cool air caressing my heated skin, and I felt the button on my jeans loosen. I bit at his bottom lip and he growled, and damn, if that wasn't the sexiest sound I'd ever heard. I reached for the hem of his shirt, but he slipped away.

"Hey," I pouted, crossing my arms over my chest. Two could play that game. If he wouldn't let me see him undressed, he wouldn't see me, either.

A huff of laughter escaped him. "Patience, remember?"

Tugging at my jeans, he slipped them off my legs and tossed them on the floor, then each sock followed them. He studied my toes for a moment until I started to feel self-conscious about them and tried to pull them away. It didn't work. He held firm and kissed the tip of each toe on both feet.

"Has anyone ever told you that you have adorable toes?"

I threw my head back and laughed. "I can't say they have, but thanks, I guess?"

Suddenly, a jolt of unexpected desire lit my body up as he plunged his tongue between my toes. I yelped and tried to pull my foot away, but it worked about as well as it had the first time. He continued his assault on my foot, watching me, gauging my reactions. My clit was throbbing already, and I resisted the urge to slip my hand down there and take care of myself while he sucked on my toes.

"That's so weird," I complained, falling back onto the bed.

His teeth flash in another quick grin. "Don't like that?"

"No, it's weird that I do." I covered my eyes with my arm and curled my hands into fists, fighting for that patience.

Rico lifted my other foot to his mouth and gave it the same treatment, but this time, he stroked my center with his thumb as he did it. A moan escaped my mouth and he chuckled. The arrogant bastard. Wait until it was my turn, which would hopefully come after he fixed the growing problem between my legs. When I felt his tongue run right down the center of the sole of my foot, I squeaked and managed not to kick him in the face when my foot jerked.

"Ticklish?"

I tried really hard to frown at him. "No."

"Mmhmm." He sank down on the bed, placing light kisses all the way up my leg as he went, licking the tiny spot on my knee where I'd nicked myself shaving. "What do you want, Kara?"

"More patience," I grumbled.

Rico barked out a laugh and licked my inner thigh. "What do you want, Kara?"

My breath hissed out between my teeth. "You, Rico."

"What do you want me to do?"

The throbbing intensified as his breath danced across my desire and I gave it to him straight, as I usually tried to do. "Lick it."

His tongue swiped once through my folds and he settled his stupid, smiling face against my thigh again. "What else?"

My eyes narrowed down at him. He was playing with me. "Make me come, Rico. Make me come hard."

"As you wish."

I totally would've called him out on that *Princess Bride* reference if I hadn't been distracted by the pressure on my clit. Damn, he was good at this. I caught myself reaching for a pillow, then remembered last time and just let myself be as noisy as I wanted. That seemed to spur him on more, and the pressure increased, pulling me closer and closer to the edge. Why wasn't he using his fingers like last time, though? Did he expect me to tell him to?

"F-fingers, Rico," I gasped. "Put your fingers in me."

He hummed in acknowledgment, and I jolted against him. Teasing my entrance first, he slipped his fingers inside, curling them to hit the spot I liked, and I moaned loudly. Damn, I was so close now. His fingers thrust in and out, his tongue swirling and torturing, and his expression told how much he was enjoying it all.

Shifting slightly, he grabbed one of my cheeks and spread it, then there was pressure of an entirely new kind. He didn't insert anything in my ass, for which I was grateful, but the added pressure, the stimulation, was overwhelming and I could barely breathe. I arched my back, pressing myself closer to him, urging him to finish it. He grabbed my leg and lifted my butt off the bed, keeping my shoulders pressed to the mattress, his mouth never stopping.

At this new angle, he spun his fingers and thrust in a new direction, keeping the pressure up in the back. The sight alone was erotic, and my insides tightened up in response. His tongue stopped swirling and, instead, started licking, flattening out. It almost looked as if he really were enjoying a sweet dessert, and I almost laughed at the thought and might have if I'd been able to speak as my orgasm crashed over me.

I shuddered hard, my voice coming out a lot louder than I had intended. He released his fingers, grabbing my ass cheeks with both hands as he continued lapping at me, but I pulled away. Rico blinked up at me, his pupils dilated with desire, and I sat up quickly, snatching his shirt up over his head. I tasted myself on his lips as I yanked his belt off, but I didn't mind so much.

His huge cock sprang free as I fought to get his pants off. Again, he tried to push me back on the bed, but I swatted his hands away, taking him into my mouth. He hissed and his hand latched onto my hair almost instantly.

"You don't have to," he said, running his fingers along my scalp.

My response was to push him back again. I released him, running my tongue along his shaft and circling the head. His eyes glazed over, which I took as a good sign. I wrapped my hand around the base and stroked, eliciting a deep groan from him. The salty taste of him made me crave more. My tongue swiped across his slit, then I swallowed him again, my hand working in time with my mouth, tongue wrapping around him.

I took him in as far as I could, careful not to choke myself on him. His muscles tensed, hips shifting up a couple of times. I could tell he was trying hard not to thrust.

"Mmm, shit, if you keep doing that, I'm going to come before I get inside you."

I laughed around him, which made his hands tighten in my hair. Finally, I let him go, crawling over him as he had me a while ago. He grabbed my face and kissed me hard, and I straddled him. Crinkling brought my attention to his hand, where he held a condom. I snatched it away and opened it, rolling it over him ever so slowly. He gripped my hips, fighting for restraint.

"Patience," I told him, smirking.

"I'll show you patience," he retorted, baring his teeth.

I pouted playfully. "You did say something about letting me take the lead anytime, right?"

His chest rumbled with that sexy growl thing he did, but his eyes were heated, and he almost looked excited. I know I was. I'd been wanting to try this since he first mentioned it.

As soon as he was secure, I grabbed him and positioned myself, sliding down as slowly as I could. Rico's eyes squeezed shut and his breathing hitched. As soon as I was fully seated, that feeling came over me again, like that was where I was meant to be. There was something on a deeper level that felt a sense of wholeness, of completion when we came together. Rico opened his eyes and something in them stirred.

I ran my hands across the ridges of his abs to brace myself on his chest, then I lifted myself up and pushed back again. Somehow, I got the sense that he was fighting to keep from taking the lead. I was the boss this time, I thought, amused. I repeated the motion again, kept it up trying to gain the same momentum he'd had, but my muscles weren't used to the motion. With that thought came the idea that his were, but I shook it away. I did *not* want to think about that.

Leaning down to kiss him, I murmured, "Take over."

"Thought you'd never ask." He growled in my ear as he rolled us and slammed into me hard.

My legs locked around his waist, and I pulled him down to me, claiming his lips as he drove us faster, his solid mass filling me so completely. Our tongues danced together, and my head spun with giddiness. Rico had no idea of the power he had over me. I hadn't let another man get this close in what seemed like ages. My chest was full to bursting with the happiness he brought out in me.

He looped my leg over one arm, pulling it up close to my chest, turning me just enough to hit a new spot. I gasped, the pleasure rolling through me, but it wasn't enough. Taking the initiative, I caught his eye, licked my fingers seductively—or, at least, I hoped that's how it looked—and jammed them between us, rubbing myself furiously. He slowed down for a moment to watch, eyes widening in fascination, until I pressed my heels into his ass.

"Harder," I demanded, my fingers circling that sensitive bundle of nerves.

Groaning, he complied, picking up his pace again. "You are so damn hot right now."

"Come with me, Rico."

He grunted something that sounded like an agreement, lifted some of his weight off of me, then grabbed one of my pillows and shoved it under my lower back. I bit down on a strangled cry as I felt another big one building. Rico was panting, watching my fingers do their work, and I could practically see him drooling. I put my other hand to work, massaging and teasing my breasts, causing his eyes to snap back up. Throwing my head back, I gasped and cried out, the edge rushing toward me.

"Shit," he cursed just as his cock stiffened even more, and he kept pounding through until I met him, and we collapsed in a heap on the bed, trying to catch our breath.

A shudder ran through me, forcing another hiss out of him as I tightened around him again. I wrapped my arms around him and rolled us to the side, pulling him close. We just lay there together for a while, breathing each other in, and it was perfect.

Chapter 16 - Rico

Morning came too soon. I studied Kara's features in the dim light as she slept, brushing a lock of hair from her face. She stirred and scooted closer, curling into me.

"I have to go home, at least to shower and change clothes." I laughed and pressed a soft kiss to Kara's forehead.

She groaned and pressed her face to my chest. "I wish you could stay."

Me too.

Valor, of course, was all for making things permanent, and even though every moment with Kara made me lean in that direction, it was a total about-face from everything I'd been planning all of my life. Get the trust fund, leave it all behind, and go somewhere no one could find me.

But the more time I spent with her, the more I recognized what I would be giving up. Would I walk away just to realize I missed it all, then come right back? I wasn't sure Kara would forgive me if I did, and that sent a pang through my chest.

After several more kisses, I finally managed to disentangle myself from Kara and headed home. The morning was nice, and though I was eager to get back to Kara, I enjoyed the scenery of the drive more than usual. To my surprise, a strange car was parked out front when I pulled up. As soon as I parked my truck in the barn and walked halfway across the yard, I smelled him.

Uncle Perry was back. Oddly enough, this time it didn't make me angry. It seemed I had gained some perspective, after all. I knew he just wanted to make sure that I would live my best life and become the man he knew I was capable of being. If he didn't care about me, he wouldn't have come at all.

I had to appreciate having someone in my life who held me in such high regard. Flashes of Kara's voice as she talked about her parents and how they didn't even recognize her rang in my ears. Who was I to get angry at someone who was trying to help me gain access to the immense fortune my parents had left me?

So when I stepped inside and found Uncle Perry in the living room with Uncle James, I walked right up and hugged him. "It's good to see you."

Perry looked surprised, but he hugged me and clapped me on my back. "Things were quiet in Arizona, so I thought I would come by and see how you are doing."

I had to admit how well it had been going, and I couldn't keep the smile off my face. "Things are better than I ever expected. Not only here with the family, but with Kara. If I'm being honest, I'm not sure where I want to go from here, but I think my perspective has changed. I feel like I owe you both a huge thanks for giving me the kick I needed."

Perry and James beamed at me. It seemed they were thrilled with my admission, and pride swelled in my chest. "I am so proud of you," Perry said.

James chimed in. "Me too."

"And you've just got a week to go before the first part of your trial period is up." Perry ducked his head and tapped his fist lightly on my chest. "I just wanted to make sure you weren't going to fool around and fuck it up."

I burst out laughing. "No, things are going so well with the job aspect, I don't anticipate there being a problem."

Perry's face split into an even wider grin. "Son, I tell you, if things keep going this well, you might accomplish your goal sooner than we first said. This change in you, if it proves permanent..." He cleared his throat. Was he about to cry? "This change, if it's permanent, that's all we wanted."

Time to change the subject before I had to get the man a hankie. "Uncle, while you're here, I need some advice."

He straightened up and got serious. "Of course. Anything."

"It's Valor. I told Uncle James about it, but maybe you've heard something. He's trying to force the bite. I almost bit Kara, several times now. And neither of us is ready for that step. She doesn't even know about Valor." I threw up my hands. "I'm not ready to reveal this deep, dark secret yet. We've only been..." Why were these things so hard to say to my uncles? "Ah, intimate, for a couple of weeks now. It's too fast. Also, I'm pretty sure Valor has tried to project his voice into Kara's mind already."

Perry rubbed his fingers across his stubble and furrowed his brow. "What are you waiting for?"

The answer popped into my head without any thought. And it surprised me. "Love," I whispered. "I need her to love me first." That was a pretty big revelation. Not just to my family but to myself.

Finally.

Valor had known all along. Of course he had.

Perry sighed and gave me a sympathetic look. "I'm not surprised, really. You don't want her to reject you."

James's face registered amusement. "When did you turn into a psychologist?"

Perry puffed up with pride. "Hey, I took my job seriously. I still screwed it up, but I read a bunch of books about a child losing their parents when I took on the responsibility of raising Rico. I know I spoiled him too much," he shot me a severe look as if that was my fault, "but I tried to help him as much as I could. Children whose parents die young often feel abandoned and have a hard time letting potential mates get close."

My jaw dropped. His explanation made sense, and even though Kara's parents were technically still alive, her initial reluctance to get close could be explained the same way. "That…" I shook my head. "Yeah. I think that's right."

She loves you.

"I know she loves me." I answered my dragon out loud. "But there's a right way and a wrong way to do things. She hasn't admitted those feelings yet. I can't do this too soon and have her freak out."

Perry nodded. "That's smart. Make sure *she's* sure of her feelings first."

She'll respond better than you think.

I couldn't take that risk yet.

Give her hints. See how she reacts.

"Valor is suggesting I allude to the truth and see how she reacts," I relayed to my uncles.

They both agreed. "It can't hurt," James said. "Just see where the conversation goes and if she's open to the idea."

I ate lunch with Perry, but he took pity on me when I kept checking my phone. I'd told Kara I was coming home to shower and grab some clothes. She was expecting me. "Go," he laughed. "Go get your girl."

After a fast hug, I ran upstairs and took the world's fastest shower, then threw some clothes in a bag and was out the door before fifteen more minutes had passed. My truck flew down the road, back to Kara.

Back to my girl.

We spent the day around her house. She'd started doing some cleaning while I was gone, hair pulled up in an adorable messy bun. "Hey," I called over the sound of the vacuum.

Kara jumped in surprise and whirled around. "Rico!" she exclaimed. "I figured you wouldn't be back until this evening for our date."

Embarrassment colored my face. I hadn't realized she'd expected me to stay home. "I'm sorry. I can come back?"

The drone of the vacuum cut off. Kara laughed. "No, silly, you're welcome here. But I will probably put you to work."

Those were the best words she could've said. It had to mean something that she was so comfortable with me in her home that she'd make me clean it with her, right?

I volunteered to scrub the bathroom. It was cleaner than my own at the manor since I'd been spending all my time away. I hadn't had a moment to wipe it down. I eyed the tub, wondering if it would fit the both of us comfortably. Shaking that distracting thought from my head, I forced myself to focus on my task. It was hard, in more than one way.

We spent the rest of the day neatening and dusting, wiping, and teasing one another. It brought an increasingly familiar satisfaction with it, to have that level of comfort and familiarity with her. We'd planned to picnic up the trail for dinner. She took a quick shower while I made sandwiches and put them in her backpack cooler.

As we walked up the trail, enjoying the sights and sounds of the woods, we talked about this and that. And I found a way to bring up the subject. A fox screeched in the woods, sounding very much like a woman's scream. I recognized it as a sound I'd heard many times while flying, but Kara was surprised. "What was that?" she exclaimed. "It sounded like someone in trouble!"

"It's okay." I put my hands on her shoulders. "It's a fox."

Kara's shoulders slumped. "Are you sure?" She peered around my shoulders. "Will a fox hurt us?"

I chuckled and took her hand, leading her along. "You haven't spent much time in the woods?"

"Not really." She looked at me out of the corner of her eyes. "I always mean to. That's why I owned these hiking boots and that backpack. But I never seem to get around to it."

"Do you like it?" I asked.

She nodded vigorously. "I do. This is great, actually."

That was good since I spent an extraordinary amount of time in these very woods. By now I knew all the best trails, the best views. We weren't on Kingston land at the moment, so I didn't have to worry about running into a wolf or dragon and having to force the explanation before I was prepared, but we were getting close. I could smell it.

I narrowed my eyes and wiggled my fingers at her. "Maybe we'll run into a werewolf," I said in an ominous voice.

Kara burst out laughing. "I wish!"

I'd been hoping she'd say that. When we'd cleaned her house, I'd been dusting her bedroom and took a look at her bookshelf. The books were mainly about paranormal creatures, a mix of romance and fantasy. Vampires, werewolves… even some about dragon shifters.

I really wanted to read those books and see how much they got right, but I didn't want to get *caught* reading those books. The guys would never let me hear the end of it.

She looked at me suspiciously, her eyes glinting playfully. "Did you see my books?"

I burst out laughing and pulled her close with my arm around her shoulders. "Maybe."

"Well, you might as well know, I'd love to have a shifter for a husband. If we run into a werewolf in these woods, you might just lose me to him."

Valor growled deep in my chest. Kara was so close to me there was no way she couldn't hear it. "Maybe you could pick a different shifter," I suggested. "Dragons sound way cooler."

Kara sighed wistfully. "I know you're going to think I'm silly. But dragons are my favorite."

Valor's emotions changed from jealousy to preening. If he'd been shifted, he would've pranced up the trail. Hell, I felt like joining him.

Maybe Valor was right. She might take it well, knowing I turned into a dragon. But still, I didn't want to completely freak her out. "Do you think there are real paranormal beings out there?" I asked cautiously.

She didn't answer right away, but she straightened up and continued up the trail. Walking with my arm around her and her face pressed against my chest had been awkward, but I missed having her close. Damn, I had it bad.

"I think the world is too big. The universe is too vast. So while I would love to give it an absolute yes, I think probably no. More than likely, we're the only ones here. But I don't discount the possibility. There are too many mysteries in this world to give that question a hard no."

As the sun sank behind the trees, she looked up at me in curiosity. "Do *you* believe in the paranormal?"

A trail was coming up that would take us onto Kingston land. I'd chosen this particular path intentionally so that if it went well, I could move over to Kingston land and maybe shift for her. "I do think it's real," I replied seriously. "I believe in it all. Ghosts, shifters, angels and demons, the whole shebang."

I'd never seen creatures such as those, but maybe they'd never seen a being like me, either. There was no reason to think they didn't exist and every reason to think they did. Like she'd said, there were too many mysteries for a definite answer.

She laughed and squeezed my hand. "I'm glad we're on the same page."

I steered us toward the path to the Kingston land. "Do you mind walking into the dark?" I asked. "I know this area very well. We're in no danger."

She cocked her head at me and smiled. "I trust you."

My heart swelled as we moved closer and closer to a place that I'd have to put that trust to the test. If the past few minutes were anything to go on, I didn't have anything to worry about, and Valor agreed. I couldn't be sure exactly how she'd take it, but I had a feeling it wouldn't be with terror. I hoped.

We chatted about the different types of paranormal creatures until I was absolutely sure we were on my family's land. When I smelled the wolves that patrolled the perimeters, I knew we were safe as soon as we found a good spot.

It didn't take much longer. A clearing opened up off the trail. There was still plenty of daylight left, though the light had waned to something rather romantic. The clearing was scattered with some blue and bright red flowers that nearly glowed in the setting sunlight.

"Come over here," I said. "We can eat here."

Kara, after sticking her nose in some of the fragrant flowers, unpacked our sandwiches as I spread a light blanket on the soft grass. Valor hummed inside me, impatient for us to eat so he could reveal himself. I took my time, mulling over the best way to bring it back up.

But there wasn't really a good way to admit something like that, was there?

"Kara," I said as soon as we finished. "I have to talk to you about something."

Worry flashed across her face, but she masked it quickly and looked me in my eyes. "Okay."

I didn't know how else to say it but to blurt it out. "Kara, I brought up the subject of paranormal creatures and shifters for a reason. And I want you to know how much I trust you, too."

She furrowed her brow but didn't interrupt.

"I'm a shifter, Kara. I'm a dragon."

Chapter 17 - Kara

"I'm a shifter, Kara. I'm a dragon." Rico looked like he was going to stand in front of me and cry as he said those words. His expression was both serious and worried.

What was I supposed to think? He was messing with me, for sure. I laughed and shook my head as I packed up our trash. "Okay, Rico. You're a big scary dragon." We were in the middle of the woods, just out of sight of the trail, surrounded by romantic flowers. And we had this nice big blanket. I dropped my voice into a sultry tone. "Are you going to shift and bite me?" Role-playing like this would turn me on.

A lot.

If he was into it, that would be the icing on the cake. So far, he'd been everything I could've dreamed of, maybe more. If he was into this kind of role play?

My panties moistened at the thought.

"Kara." Rico took my hand and looked deep into my eyes. "Paranormal creatures are real."

His eyes flashed red for longer than a split second. I'd thought I'd seen them do that before already, but it was gone so fast I thought I was imagining things.

This time they stayed red for several seconds, plenty long enough for me to realize it wasn't just a trick of the light, and my jaw dropped. "You're being serious."

My heart froze in anticipation, then picked up double-time. Was this really happening? I licked my lips anxiously.

"I haven't read many romance novels that feature dragon shifters. Well, none, actually. So I don't know if they get it right. But I can shift into a dragon. He has his own personality separate from mine, yet at the same time, we are one. We don't always agree, and we argue sometimes, but we are together forever. You have to think of us as a package deal. As one."

One. Two consciousnesses. I'd read books like that. It was complicated, but nothing that had turned me off.

I was thinking about this as if it was real. "Prove it," I demanded. "Show me."

He stood up and stepped away from the blanket. "First, you have to know that Valor, my dragon, would never hurt you in a million years. Neither would I."

I nodded. The idea that either of them might hurt me hadn't even crossed my mind, but his reassurance warmed me. "Okay."

"It's in our nature to protect what's ours, and I'm sorry if it sounds wrong, but we think of you as ours."

My panties got twice as wet. "Okay," I whispered. I had to swallow a huge lump in my throat before the word would come out.

Rico pulled his shirt over his head. "I have to be naked," he explained. My eyes lingered over his sculpted chest as he unbuttoned his jeans and slid them down his thighs with his underwear. When he looked up and saw my gaze lingering, his dick twitched and hardened. I hummed appreciatively and pressed my fingertips to my lips to hide the grin.

And then… it happened. I blinked several times as Rico's body changed, morphing into an enormous black dragon with scales that shone in the almost-gone evening light. "Oh, my goodness." I scrambled to my feet and gawked at him.

I had to rub my eyes and think back to the day. I hadn't had a drop to drink. I didn't feel like I'd been slipped any drugs, no hallucinogens, no sleeping pills or anything. I crossed my arms and pinched myself under the arm where it really hurt to make sure I was fully awake.

I was. And a dragon still stood in front of me, staring at me with big, golden eyes. "Oh." What was I supposed to say?

Laughter bubbled up my chest. I stared at the ten-foot-long dragon and laughed.

Do I look funny?

Rico's voice resonated through my head. I choked mid-laugh, and my bubbling delight turned a bit wonky. He'd just talked to me in my head. "Rico?" I gasped.

I am Valor.

Holy shit. I was totally freaking out. I probably should've been scared, but I felt anything but.

Excitement, euphoria, adrenaline. So much adrenaline. My hands shook with it.

Deep inside, a little voice said I should be upset and scared, but I barely heard it over my internal shrieks of excitement. I wanted to pet his scales and ride him through the clouds.

"How is this possible?" I whispered, but my voice grew louder with every question. "How many of you are there? Is this real? Can I touch you? Who all knows about this? Can you breathe fire?"

A deep, throaty chuckle floated into my head. *In order. Just because you don't understand it doesn't make it unreal. There are more of us than I could count on the planet. All the male Kingstons. Yes, this is real. I believe humans call it a 'need to know' basis. And only under extreme duress can I breathe fire.*

I had to bite my tongue to keep from squealing.

I would be honored if you touched me.

My throat caught my breath and my extreme excitement flatlined into ecstasy. "How can I hear you in my head? Can you talk to others like that?"

Only other dragons. And my fated mate.

Okay, so he couldn't just speak to anyone. Only other dragons and… Wait. He just said— Holy shit. "Fated mate?" I'd read enough paranormal to know exactly what a fated mate was.

Yes.

"Are you sure?" I whispered as I stepped forward a few inches.

If it were not true, you couldn't hear me.

Laughter bubbled up my throat again, excited, borderline hysterical. "Fated mate. I'm your fated mate."

And Rico's.

Rico. Oh, for fuck's sake. Rico. My employee. My lover. My temporary employee and the best lover I've ever had. The one who was moving away after a year to live in solitude with his fortune.

And I was his fated mate. That sobered me a bit.

Valor stepped toward me as a deep rumble emitted from his chest, the same sexy one I recognized from my time with Rico. Had it been Valor doing that through him all along?

I had a fated mate, but that was some deep shit I'd figure out later. For now, I had a *real freaking dragon* standing right in front of me. The urge to run my hands over him was overwhelming. I needed physical proof to keep my mind grounded.

Tentatively, I walked toward the dragon. Toward Valor. "You're real."

He didn't speak in my head, but he ducked his head as I got close. Blinking, he crouched low. I knew he wouldn't hurt me. I giggled again as my fingers brushed the back of Valor's head and felt the smooth scales that were also somehow as hard as rock. The big, black dragon growled and pushed his head harder into my hand.

My hands continued to shake with disbelief and nothing short of pure rapture as Valor rubbed against me like a cat. The low rumbling in his chest sounded like a purr, and I was grinning so hard my face started to hurt. This was so crazy, so freaking unbelievable!

"Can I ride you?" I blurted. Then it dawned on me that might've been a rude question. "Oh, I'm sorry. Was that too forward?"

Valor pushed closer, nearly knocking me off my feet. I squealed in laughter and threw my arms around him. *Yes, you can ride me, but we should take it slow to start.*

"Yeah, of course." I walked around him, touching him, running my hands all over, his back, his tail. The long, black tail thumped the ground happily after I touched the tip.

I chose you. As soon as I smelled you in the bar the first time, even before I or Rico saw you. I knew.

He knew, somehow, that Rico and I would be the perfect companions to each other. And his dragon. Dragon.

Holy shit. The Kingstons. They were all shifters. "Is the dragon gene, or whatever, does it come out in men only?"

That is a mystery we do not understand. The gene does not pass to women.

"Amongst all shifters everywhere?" I asked as I rounded Valor and looked him in the eye again.

He cocked his head. *I do not know.*

Fair enough. I couldn't have expected one dragon to know it all, especially where other shifters were concerned. I certainly didn't know everything there was to know about human physiology. "I expect I'll learn more, won't I?"

He chuckled, and even though he didn't speak out loud, I recognized it as amusement. *Are you well, mate?*

I couldn't stop the laughter. "My legs are wobbly," I whispered.

Sit down.

Sounded like a good idea. I sank into the soft grass and found I'd moved around so I was back on the blanket again. "I want you to tell me about yourself," I whispered. "Please."

He began to speak in my head and tell me about the history of the dragons, but I was ashamed to admit that it didn't really sink in. The only thing I was able to focus on in all my elation was the cadence of his voice. The melodic nature of his tones lulled me and calmed my racing heart.

Feel better?

I sucked in a deep breath and nodded, realizing that just listening to his voice had helped tremendously. "I do." Looking up at Valor, I smiled. "What does this mean for us?"

When you're ready, Rico will bite you during sex. It will create a bond between the three of us. Your life will be extended.

Excellent, I'd get a long life. That was certainly a nice perk. This was like I'd woken up in an alternate universe. "Does it—the bite, I mean—will it hurt?"

As far as I know, it does not. Each dragon gives the bite to only one person in their life. I've never spoken to another dragon about it directly, though. It's a very private, intimate experience.

"I imagine that's true. But still, you haven't heard of any pain?"

Valor shook his head and laid his head down flat on the ground in front of me. We stared at each other without talking—internally or otherwise—for a long time. I laid my hand on his nose, feeling the silkiness of his scales, studying the texture beneath my fingers. By the time the sky had darkened to the point that I didn't think we could see to get home, I felt a strong connection with the beast.

"It's too dark to walk back," I told Valor. "Unless you can see in the dark."

Are you up to that flight?

He snuffed at me, and somehow, I knew to interpret the sound as both pleased and challenging. I didn't mind taking that challenge on. I'd see firsthand what a dragon could really do.

I grinned and nodded. "Of course."

Get on my back. Put your feet in front of my wing joints.

I did as he said and leaned forward, my feet tucked under his wings. When he spread them, I found it was surprisingly comfortable. I held on the best I could, the anticipation making my stomach flutter.

Valor took off running across the clearing and flapped his wings. A cross between a scream and squeal built in my throat as he got off the ground. He swung his wings rapidly to gain height and we cleared the trees.

When we broke above the tree line, I gasped. The night was clear and cool. The wind pulled my hair back as Valor flew, giving me a clear line of sight. He straightened out several feet above the trees and flew steadily for a while. After a few minutes, I felt brave enough to let go and sit up straight, eventually pulling my hands into the air as the wind rushed over them like wings. I was freaking flying!

Talk about a head rush. "This is amazing!" I screamed.

Valor chuckled in my head, and all too soon told me to grab hold again. As soon as I did, he began to descend in slow, wide circles, eventually landing in the backyard of a huge manor house.

The Kingston Manor.

That made sense. It was huge and old. And expensive. I didn't catch a lot of the features in the dark, but several golden lights shining through the windows lit up some of the beautiful interior and the carefully maintained lawn.

I climbed carefully down, my limbs shaking slightly from the excitement.

It has been my honor.

Valor nudged my midriff, then began to change. Seconds later, Rico stood naked in front of me with a huge, shit-eating grin on his face. "Well?" he asked.

I threw my hands around his neck and hugged him close. "That was amazing!" I purred in his ear. I quickly realized he was still naked. "Your clothes! And our picnic stuff."

"I'll go get it later," he assured me. "Give me five, and I'll change." He jogged over to a small building that looked a lot like a pool house, but there was no pool. When he came out, he wore casual clothes. Baggy basketball shorts, a tee, and flip-flops.

The enormity of the night began to wear on me, and I yawned. "We're nowhere near my truck," I said. "And I'm exhausted."

"Come on. You can stay here." He motioned toward the house and grabbed my hand, leading us toward the back door. "Uncle James and Aunt Carla aren't here."

"How do you know?" I asked.

He tapped his ears, then his nose. "I'd know."

Oh, yeah. "So you have advanced senses even when not...scaly?"

He chuckled and pulled me close, kissing the tip of my nose. "Yeah. Come on."

We walked into the house together. My mind still reeled with the information I'd absorbed all evening, but it was a great feeling. And Rico had a huge grin on his face. No doubt he'd thought I'd react badly. They always did in the books. That's probably why he'd seemed so nervous at first. He'd put a lot of trust in me, sharing his and his family's secret.

Rico pulled his covers back and I slid into the bed gratefully. My adrenaline was crashing hard, and I felt like I was going to pass out. I settled into his soft pillows, yawning again.

"Are you still you?" I asked sleepily.

"I haven't changed. You just know more about me." He curled around me and tucked my hair behind my ears before pulling the covers over me. "Even in my dragon form, when it's Valor, it's still me."

"That's all I needed to know." My eyes kept closing of their own accord until I couldn't force them open anymore and I dropped into a dreamless sleep.

Chapter 18 - Rico

I made it. It was the last day of the sixth week. I should get my first allowance from the trust fund today. It may have started off a little shaky, but I had made it to the first milestone.

I still needed to keep my job for six months to get half my inheritance in a lump sum, and another twelve months to get it all, but it was a start. A great start.

Calling out sick would've been the first thing I considered doing six weeks ago. But Kara had a full day of work today, and she'd need my help. She'd been taking on more and more jobs since there were two of us. Alone, she'd always end her day exhausted and overworked.

Kara's acceptance of me had put me at ease, far beyond what I'd known I'd been stressing about. I'd grown sure that I wanted to take her as my mate, and she seemed more than willing. In fact, she'd been delighted. I couldn't have been more relieved to have her laugh. The amazed and thrilled look on her face… I couldn't describe the weight it took off my shoulders. But claiming Kara came with its own set of new hurdles.

It meant not leaving Black Claw. It also meant finding a permanent job. As much as I liked working with Kara, it wasn't what I wanted to do forever, and she could've been apprenticing someone who actually did want to work in this field.

I was fairly sure Uncle Perry and Gramps would let me transfer from working the rest of the year to getting a degree.

That was why I'd taken the morning off. My inheritance meant I didn't have to work another day in my life past that twelve-month mark, but after working with Kara and seeing the difference a hard day's work made, I knew I couldn't go back. I needed purpose.

And it was nice to be needed. The look of delight on the client's face when we turned up to fix their problem was rewarding. I wanted more of that.

As I walked out to my truck to head to the appointment I'd made for the morning, my phone rang.

Gramps. "Morning," I said cheerily.

"Congratulations, my boy!" Gramps sounded excited. "You made it."

"I did. It was much easier than I thought it would be."

He chuckled. "I hoped once you started down the path of righteousness, you'd see it's the best way."

Righteousness. Only Gramps. "You got it." I smiled and unlocked my truck.

"Rico, I put a little something extra in your account with your first allowance payment. A gift from me to you for finding your mate. I'm so happy for you."

"Thanks," I said with real appreciation. "I might just spend it on her."

His laughter made me warm. He was truly happy for me. I'd made him proud.

It was as if I'd read his mind. "You've made me so incredibly proud, Rico."

When we hung up, I logged in and checked my bank balance before pulling out of the barn. Damn. He had been serious. It was a nice bonus from Gramps. My first instinct was to blow it on something stupid, but after a moment's hesitation, I decided to save it all.

Maybe Kara would like a nice engagement ring eventually. I'd want to get her a good one. We were still so early, but I knew, deep in my heart, she was it for me. I was already head over heels in love with her.

My appointment was at the community college the next town over. Jury had gotten his associates there, and Maddox had started off there as well. They had several technical programs that I was interested in, and I'd made an appointment with a counselor to narrow down my focus and pick one.

The counselor was very helpful, and by the end of the appointment, I felt really good about my decision to go with welding.

It was a great skill. I could use it for a job, or if I wanted, I could use it for art.

Hey, I could be artistic.

I didn't officially sign up, but I left with brochures and the certainty that I wanted to do it. On the way back to the office, my optimism rose. Valor hummed within me, finally content that I'd gotten my life on the track he wanted.

Only now, it was the track I wanted as well.

When I pulled into the office parking lot, only an hour later than normal, I knew something was wrong before I got out of the car. Kara was inside the office, but she was projecting enough anxiety to put Valor on edge.

I slammed my truck door shut and sprinted to the office. When I walked in, my jaw dropped. The place was completely wrecked.

The scent of the person that did it filled my nose. I knew who it was without a doubt. It was Tye, along with someone whose scent I didn't recognize. The question was, why?

Kara stood in the middle of the room with the stun gun I'd gotten her out and pointed aimlessly at the floor. "There's nobody here now," she said dully. "I just got here."

By the scent, they'd done it in the night. I stepped forward, over a pile of ruined office supplies, and gathered her in my arms. Tears rolled down her cheeks. "Why would anyone do this?"

I soothed her and tried to keep Valor under control. Of course, he wanted to find Tye and disembowel him.

That sure did sound like fun, but we had to play the game the human way since Tye was wholly unremarkable and human, even if he was a prick.

"It had to be personal," she whispered into my chest. "I don't keep money here. And I don't think anything was stolen, just destroyed."

The tools had oil poured all over them. They'd clean, but it would be a bitch. Anything that could be broken was destroyed. Glass on the floor, plastic bins smashed, papers everywhere. I pulled out my phone without letting go of Kara and texted our family group chat. I wasn't sure who was on duty at the police station, but everyone except Maddox worked for them. One of them would come.

It was James and Maverick, luckily. They replied they'd be here soon.

In the meantime, I bundled Kara up in my truck and stood beside her with the door open and my arms around her. "Does someone hate me that much?"

"No," I admonished her gently. "This isn't somebody hating you for being a woman in this field. This was personal."

She sniffed and nodded as James and Maverick pulled into the lot in the cruiser. "Be right back," I whispered. "You start messaging the people we were supposed to work for today and let them know we can't come." She started to protest, but I raised my eyebrows. She was in no condition to work.

Finally, she nodded. "Okay. Yeah, I think that's probably best."

When my uncle and cousin stepped out of the cruiser, I pulled them to the side. "I told you about Tye," I whispered, shooting my eyes toward Kara to make sure she was okay. They both nodded. "I smell him all over the place in there, along with another smell I don't recognize."

"We'll figure it out," James said. "Does she have a statement to give us? Anything that could help us nail this bastard?"

I shook my head. "No, and she didn't touch anything but the front door."

"Good." Maverick nodded at Kara. "Get her out of here. We'll get someone from the wolf pack in to clean up once we've gotten all the information we need from the scene."

I gave him a quick hug in appreciation and clapped James on the back. "Thanks. I owe you both one."

I walked back to my truck and pressed my lips to Kara's forehead briefly before closing the door and hurrying around to the driver's side. Hopping behind the wheel, we left the red and blue cruiser lights in the rearview. Kara had settled into a tense silence, staring out the window. Her hands were clasped together in her lap, knuckles white.

I reached over and lightly tugged at her arm. She relinquished her death grip and let me fold my fingers into hers. I pulled her hand to my mouth and kissed it, then settled it between us.

"Would it be a bad time to tell you who did it?" I asked hesitantly.

Emerald eyes snapped to me. "How could you know something like that? You weren't there."

"They left a scent." I tapped my nose with the hand that held hers.

"Oh. Right." She nodded distractedly. "Do I know—no, of course, I do, or you wouldn't have asked. Who was it, Rico? Who did that?" Her voice carried an edge of retribution. It was hot.

I glanced over and found her watching me intently. "Tye, and one other scent I wasn't sure about. Maybe one of his buddies from the bar that night."

Her eyebrows pulled together in a frown. "But, why? Why is he bothering me now?"

The question sounded rhetorical, so I tightened my grip on her hand and let her mull it over. My theory, and it was the most likely scenario, was that jealousy played a big hand in it. After that night at the bar, the way he'd been pressed against her, the bruise he'd left on her, it took everything I had not to go after him. Now, though, he'd kicked himself several notches up on my priority list, right after I saw to my woman.

Claim her. Make her ours.

"Ow." Kara hissed, jerking her hand away and shaking it.

"Shit, I'm sorry," I quickly apologized. I slowly loosened my grip on the protesting steering wheel before I accidentally ripped it off the column. "Just thinking about that bastard—"

She shook her head and grabbed my arm. "No, it's fine, I get it. If I knew where he was now, I'd love to go and pop him right in the skull, too." Definitely hot.

I cracked a smile at the ferocity in her voice. Obviously, I kept it hidden—I wasn't suicidal. When we got to her place, I went straight for the bathroom and flipped the water on. Under the sink, I found bubble bath and threw a splash or two in the tub, then let it fill.

When I walked out, she was curled into a ball in the corner of the couch, her arms wrapped around her legs as if she was trying to keep them from running out the door. I grabbed a couple of candles from the kitchen counter and set them in the bathroom. I rifled through a few of the cabinets and drawers, then moved for the bedroom.

"What are you looking for?" she asked.

"More candles." I grinned at her reassuringly.

Kara lifted her head, tilting it slightly. "What for?" I guess she couldn't hear the water running out here as I could.

Grinning, I replied, "You're supposed to have candles with bubble baths, right?"

I ducked into her bedroom, snagged the candles I'd seen on her dresser, and then found her staring at my handiwork in progress in the bathroom. Setting them out as neatly as I could, I lit them with a lighter I'd found in the kitchen and flipped the light switch, letting the orange glow dominate the small space.

I slipped my phone from my pocket and opened up my favorite music app, scrolling through until I found something she liked. Setting it on the edge of the sink, I turned back to her.

She grabbed my shirt and pulled me into her, our lips crashing together like waves on the shore. I slid my hand to the back of her head, tugging as gently as I could at the hair tie until her silky brown tresses tumbled loosely around her shoulders. I loved it when it was down. Soft, pliant lips parted, and her teeth grazed my jaw, nipped at my ear. Her fingers explored beneath my shirt, so I removed it for her.

"Why are you so good to me?" she whispered against my skin.

I curled my finger under her chin, bringing her gaze up to mine. "Because I love you." The words came easily without even a second thought, and instead of feeling nervous like I thought I might have, I felt secure in my own feelings, for once.

Blinking tears back, she caught my mouth again. Fingers traced the sensitive skin at my waistband, and then she was tossing my belt on the floor. I tugged her shirt off and kissed a line from the corner of her mouth to her earlobe, where I set my teeth to the delicate flesh. She gasped, arms snaking around my neck. "I love you, too," she said in a sure voice. "But I'm so glad you said it first."

Laughing and groaning, I pressed my forehead to hers. "Then I'll say it again. I love you." As she continued exploring my body, I looked at the bubble bath and sighed. "I had every intention of setting this up for you so you could relax and destress."

She loosened my jeans and shoved her hand inside, grabbing my already stiffened length. "This destresses me better," she said, stroking once, twice. "Get in the tub."

My pants fell to the floor, but I held onto her hand around me, making both of us pump again. "Whatever you want."

Her gaze dropped to her hand, watching intensely, but then swept back up to mine. "Only you, Rico. I only want you."

The wall was cold on my skin when she pushed me up against it, and I almost tripped over the pants still around my ankles, then glorious warmth wrapped around my length and it was all I could do to remain standing. This was not at all what I had in mind. I wanted to make her feel good, to make her come and come again until she begged me to stop.

I understood it, though. Her space had been invaded thoroughly, and she needed to feel in control again. What more control could a woman want than to have a man naked and at her mercy, the possibility of using either her tongue for pleasure or her teeth for untold pain? It was a terrifying thought, and yet sparks danced under my skin watching her hand and mouth work in sync with the music blaring from my phone.

Her other hand cupped my balls and my breath puffed out excitedly. Damn, she was gonna make me finish too soon. I needed to stop her. I needed to please her.

I needed to shut the water off.

"Shit!"

I reached for the handles, but Kara pressed her palm to my stomach, holding me still, her head bobbing faster in time with the beat. Damn it! My fingers found her hair, but she smacked them away, so I pressed them to the cool wall. It was nearly impossible to keep my hips still, her soft whimpers like the most erotic music. When she groaned, the vibration sent a jolt all the way up into my stomach and back.

"Kara, stop or I'm gonna—"

Her hand pressed harder against me and I banged my head on the wall. This woman was going to be my undoing—or rather, she already was. I loved Kara. I loved her smile, her laugh, her attitude. I loved her green eyes and the smell of her skin. I loved the way she made me want to be a better person. God, I loved her *tongue*.

My eyes squeezed shut as she shoved me over the brink. "Hnng, Kara!" I gasped.

This time, when my fingers latched onto her hair, she didn't swat them away. I felt her throat working, pulling every ounce from me, and my hips took over as my brain shorted out. She grunted in surprise as I pumped into her mouth twice, then she sat back, licking at the tip one more time. Smiling up at me, a smug look in her eyes, she reached over and shut off the water, which was looking dangerously full.

She must've sensed my thought because she said, "The bubbles make it look more than it is. See?"

Scooping a handful out, I noticed the water was at a much more reasonable level than I'd thought. Then the pink bubbles were on my cock. I raised an eyebrow at her, and she shrugged innocently.

"I'm pretty sure I told you to get in the tub," she said.

"Mmm, yes, ma'am."

I fished a condom out of my jeans pocket and did as she commanded, lowering myself into the hot water. Kara stood, smirking down at me. Yeah, I was sitting in pink bubbles. So what? Then she undressed very, very slowly, to the beat of the music still pulsing around us. My mouth watered as her jeans slid down, and she turned her ass to me when she bent to shimmy them down her legs. *That* was a nice view. I hurriedly ripped the package open.

As soon as she freed her feet, I reached out and grabbed her hips, dragging that fine ass to my face. She squeaked and grabbed the toilet lid for balance as my tongue slid across my favorite place. I flicked over her clit and stroked hard across her opening before diving straight into forbidden territory.

"Ah!" she cried, jerking away reflexively. "What the hell?"

"Thought I'd give it a shot," I answered, grinning. "No?"

She turned her head to glare at me, but there was no heat in it. "No. At least, not yet. That's just weird."

I ran my hand across her lower back, easing her down a little more, and my tongue went to work on her delicious folds. Keeping one hand on her ass, I wrapped the other around myself under the bubbles, stroking gently. Every time she moaned, my grip tightened. It seemed she'd gotten around that noise barrier quickly.

Suddenly, the pressure on my mouth was gone and she climbed into the tub before I could protest. Her back faced me, and I grabbed her hips to steady her as she lowered herself into the water. I pulled my knees to the sides, keeping her legs together as she crouched and eased down onto me. Oh, if I'd thought her tight before, this was downright constrictive. A hiss of pleasure escaped me, and I pressed my head hard against the wall.

Using the sides of the tub as leverage, she slowly moved up and down, getting a feel for it. She hummed when I jerked up into her, but she shot me a warning look over her shoulder. I chuckled, moving my grip from her hips to her breasts, pressing her back against me. My mouth found her neck and I tested my teeth on it, just lightly. Valor roared at me to do it, and it took enormous effort to restrain that instinct. Kara, however, shuddered at the contact.

"Do that again," she whispered. She was building to a good rhythm, the bubbles rolling around us in waves.

Her request sent a shiver down my spine, and I set my teeth to her shoulder, putting a little more pressure on her skin. She cursed aloud, her pace picking up sloppily. Valor thrashed and I had to let go before I did something she wasn't ready for yet.

"Rico," Kara whimpered. "P-please."

I took the hint and knocked one leg out from under her. She fell back against me, and I grabbed her other leg and pulled it up on the ledge, bracing my shoulders and feet against either end of the tub. My free hand plunged back into the water and went to town on her clit as I slammed into her, the water sloshing violently. In the small space of the bathroom, her cries were almost deafening even over my phone speaker, and pride stretched a fierce grin across my face.

"Yea—yes, Rico!"

She clamped down on me harder, and I knew I wouldn't last much longer. Her hand grabbed mine and directed my movements, and damn, if that wasn't hot. Kara had really surprised me in that aspect, and I'd discovered that it was a major turn-on to watch her participate in her own pleasure. She knew what she liked, and she wasn't afraid to say it. It was how we'd gotten to this point after I'd issued the challenge to give her the best sex of her life and she vowed to test it.

Kara threw her head back on my shoulder and gasped, our folded fingers sliding back and forth across her clit. I picked up the pace again, determined to follow her, my release building rapidly. My nose buried in her hair, the sweet scent of her flooding my senses, the edge finally rushed up to meet me.

Chapter 19 - Kara

We spent Monday catching up on Friday's jobs and cleaning up the office. Bless Rico's heart, he'd had someone come in and clean most of it up. We just had to reorganize and make a report for the insurance company.

And he'd had security cameras overnighted. While I organized and made lists, he installed them.

I had to admit, they were pretty fancy. They blended in with the shelves of tools. "They stream directly into the cloud," Rico explained as I studied one. "So, even if a thief comes in and finds them and disables them, they can't get to the recordings to erase them."

Rico beamed at me.

"This is amazing." I looked around my clean, secure office before throwing my arms around Rico. "Are you sure you're going into the right line of work?"

He furrowed his brow at me. "What do you mean?"

I indicated the security cameras. "I mean, you were all over this. I know you don't want to go into law enforcement, but Rico, you have a unique perspective."

His arched eyebrow prompted me to continue.

"You used to be…" Damn, how did I say it without sounding judgmental? "Sort of a delinquent, or criminal, right?"

I winced when he stepped back and studied me, but he nodded in agreement. "Not sort of. I did some shady, shitty stuff."

"But you don't anymore." I took his hand and squeezed it hopefully. "Yet, you have some insight into that world. Why don't you consider going into security? You could set up security systems, figure out where the vulnerabilities are, that whole shebang. Lots of businesses want to go high tech with their security. Why not?"

His jaw dropped. "Kara, that sounds perfect. I would never have thought of that! I could take some computer classes and some criminal investigation type."

I shrugged. "You don't necessarily need a full degree. Just increase your knowledge base. Hell, you could even teach some self-defense classes." I'd be the first to sign up.

He snorted and shook his head. "Half the women in town would sign up just to learn from a Kingston." He said his last name in a mocking voice and used air quotes.

I gave him a fake jealous look. "Maybe I'll sit in on those classes."

He whirled me around the office in a tight hug. "I was okay with doing welding. But this makes me excited. This feels right, Kara. And it's all thanks to you."

The kiss he gave me curled my toes. "If that's the thanks I get, I'll have to come up with more bright ideas." I bumped my forehead to his. "Think of it as thanks for fixing up my office."

I looked around again, reminded that my personal space had been horribly violated, and I felt anger bubbling up again. "Did they get him?"

Rico shook his head. "No. And there's no physical proof that we can use for a human court. All we have is smell. He was smart about it, which likely means this isn't his first rodeo. No fingerprints. Nobody saw him. No stray hairs, even. Jury would've been able to home in on actual physical evidence if there was any."

That was a scary thought. I sighed. "I doubt he'll come back and try something like this again. He knows we're on to him."

Rico didn't seem as sure. "I'm going to go fix that thermostat at Beth's office," he reminded me. "What else is on the agenda?"

I double-checked the app. "Actually, we have a light day today. One cancellation and Beth is the only other job. I think I'll use the time to go to the grocery store. You're eating me out of house and home." I winked at him to show I didn't mind one bit.

But his face blanched. "Oh my gosh, I'm such an idiot. I wasn't even thinking. Dragons eat a *lot*." He pulled out his wallet. "First of all, stop paying me."

I arched an eyebrow at him. "Um. No. You're working. I'll pay you."

Rico grinned cheekily. "Kara, babe. I'm only working here because I want to. I made it to my six weeks. I have an allowance now that is probably quadruple what you pay me."

I knew what he meant but didn't pass up the chance to tease him. "So, you're too good for my money?" I drew up in pretend outrage. "How dare you!"

Rico's face fell, then he squinted his eyes at me. "Your face says angry, but your emotional mood is teasing."

"My emotional mood?" What in the world? He could sense something like that?

At my expression, he clarified. "We aren't bonded yet, but I can sort of… feel your feelings." He shrugged. "It's a perk."

I dropped the act. "Oh, fine then. I won't pay you. Are you sure, though?"

He nodded. "Yes. And I'm going to talk to my family about letting me switch from working for you to going to school. I've got to do a lot of research about security system management, maybe some sort of PI type setup. I don't know yet. I need my laptop and a good, long day on the internet."

"Well, it's good we're slow. You go do that. I'll fix Beth's thermostat in a jiffy. I'm almost positive it just needs a battery."

He chuckled. "That's what I thought." Sticking his hand behind him, he pulled a nine-volt out of his back pocket. "It's not hard-wired into the electrical and needs batteries. I noticed when we replaced her condenser and I had to turn it off."

"Good eye." He didn't want to do this sort of stuff all his life, but he was good at it. Hey, if we were fated mates, at least it meant I'd have a helper if I ever needed one. "Rico." I began a conversation that had been bugging me. "Tell me about the bonding process."

He looked up in surprise. "Sure. Um, it happens during sex. I will bite you, usually on the neck. It doesn't hurt."

That had been my next question. "Will it heal?"

"Yes, quickly. It will create a bond between us. You'll have an extended life, and we'll both know when the other is in distress. And other emotions, so I'm told."

I nodded and considered his words. It sounded exactly like in the romance books. Some of these authors had to have known what it was like or have gone through it themselves.

"Start looking for a replacement for me." He pulled me into his arms again. "I'll still go on jobs with you as long as I'm not working on my new thing. Or school, or whatever comes of this. But you need a real apprentice, someone who can benefit from this job as much as you will." He squeezed me tight. "And hopefully a woman."

I laughed and nodded. "You got it." I was so happy to see the light in his eyes. I knew the gears were turning as he already tried to figure out how it would work.

After I hurried him out the door, I took one last look at my newly cleaned office. I still had a lot to do.

And I still didn't understand why Tye did this. Was it because I had rejected him at the bar? Had Rico roughing him up done that much damage to his psyche? Maybe his pride was hurt? So why not go after Rico instead of me?

"Hey!" Rico stuck his head back inside. "Keep your guard up. You've got your stun gun?"

I nodded and patted my cross-body bag. "I switched purses and I promise not to take this one off."

"Good. There's no telling where that bastard's head is at." He blew me a kiss and left for real this time.

When I got in my truck, a couple of $100 bills were in the console with a note on a ripped piece of paper. "For keeping me fed." He'd drawn a complicated picture of a dragon winking. How had he done that so fast?

His little note kept a smile on my face all through Beth's house. She wasn't home, which was lucky for me or it would've taken three times as long to finish the job. We would've been talking the whole time.

But when I pulled into the grocery store parking lot, I remembered the feeling I'd had in the parking lot the last time I was here. Now I knew it had to have been Tye making me feel so on edge that day.

I got out of the truck and hurried inside. I didn't have that feeling of being watched again, but my nerves were shot. And I had a lot to buy. It didn't look like Rico planned to spend any less time at my place.

And I didn't want him to.

That meant I had to start shopping for two. Big difference.

He'd texted me several things he wanted to have on hand as I switched the battery at Beth's and drove back to town. I sought them out first, then went on to my list.

Picking out a tomato was a serious business to me. I loved tomatoes, but only if they were perfectly ripe—and not too ripe. As I stood in front of the display, poking and smelling the red balls, I kept shooting furtive glances around, trying to stay alert as I focused on my food.

When someone said my name behind me, I jumped and dropped my tomato, narrowly catching it again before it hit the floor.

Oh, yeah, I was on fire. A real kick-ass lady. I whirled around to find Cynthia behind me. Great.

She rolled her eyes and scoffed. "You were always so dramatic. What's got you so skittish?"

I sighed and went back to my tomatoes. "It's just been a long day. What do you want?" I glanced back at her to find her smiling as if being friendly.

It didn't fool me. Don't think I missed the mean girl look in her eyes. It was there, loud and proud. "Oh, I was just curious about Rico," she said. She tapped one manicured nail on her lip. "Is it something real? Or is he another one of your flings to pretend you aren't a total lezbo?"

In my head, I counted to five before replying. If I hadn't, I would've smashed the tomato in her face, and even though Rico's uncle was the police chief, I didn't want him having to get me out of trouble.

"Oh, I bet it's him," she said in a wondering voice. "He's using you to pass the time and you're letting him. Let's face it. You haven't had dick that hot since Tye doodled you one time in high school."

My blood boiled and my face went as red as the tomato, but I was *not* stooping to Cynthia's level. "Get over it, Cynthia. You're just jealous that he won't look at you twice. He's taken now, and he's happy about it."

She sniffed and stuck her nose up. "He'll figure out that he could do much better. Of all the women who ended up with a Kingston man, you're the least of them."

Doubts instantly plagued me, even as I told myself Cynthia was just doing what she'd always done. "Are you finished?" I asked harshly. "I have food to shop for. You know, for Rico?"

I tossed my hair over my shoulder and grabbed several tomatoes at random.

"Of course," Cynthia replied in a sickeningly sweet voice. "It's just going to be such a shame seeing your face all sad again when he leaves you. You'll be all alone again. When he goes back home, you know, as he's planned to all along."

How would she know anything about that? Valor chose me. Rico chose me. He wasn't leaving me. But Cynthia saw she'd struck a nerve and kept pushing. "Surely you knew that he planned to go back to Arizona and work for his grandfather?" she asked. "If you're so close, he would've told you that already."

"Fuck off, Cynthia." I walked away and left Cynthia in the produce section, her giggles invading my head. I kept telling myself that Cynthia was a bitter has-been. She was popular in high school, and her family was rich. But when she didn't go to college as they'd wanted her to, and then she didn't marry the popular, successful man she expected to, she'd had to resort to dead-end jobs to make ends meet. The whole town had talked about her family cutting her off until she grew up.

She still hadn't. She was the same spoiled brat, but now she had nothing to lose.

Yet still, as I finished my shopping, still trying to be alert, scenarios of Rico leaving kept flashing through my mind.

Hell, I'd encouraged him to start self-defense classes. What if he met someone? I knew Valor had chosen me, but that didn't mean he couldn't choose someone else. He hadn't bitten me, after all. We'd had sex since he shifted for me and he hadn't done it yet, even though I'd made it clear I wanted it.

I told him I loved him. He said he loved me.

But Cynthia knew that Rico had planned to leave. I was pretty sure he'd changed his mind, but he hadn't actually come out and said he planned to stay in Black Claw. I didn't want to move away. My foster father and sister were the only family I ever had. Until Rico, they were the only people I had in the world. No way I'd leave them after they chose me and brought me into their lives and their hearts.

I might've gotten everything on my list, but probably didn't. Regardless, I headed for the checkout. The only thing I wanted now was to talk to Rico and get it straight from him, while he looked me in the eye, that he had no intention of leaving Black Claw.

I remembered to be alert and kept looking all around as I threw the groceries in the back of the truck. No hairs stood on end, and I didn't get that watched feeling. But I couldn't get my mind off of every conversation Rico and I had ever had, searching for a moment he might've mentioned staying in Black Claw.

He'd talked about enrolling in the local community college but hadn't done it yet. Nothing meaningful had happened, besides him showing Valor to me. But who was to say that wasn't a fleeting fancy that made him do it? How much did I *really* know about Rico?

By the time I got home and got my groceries loaded in my arms, my mind was in a frenzy. I hadn't had anxiety like this since I graduated high school and got away from those assholes. I'd been on medication for it but had stopped taking it a few years ago as I needed it less and less often.

I was already in the back door and had hauled all the bags up onto the kitchen island before I realized the front door was standing wide open. How had I not seen that?

Dropping the bags as fast as I could get them off my arms, I scrambled against the counter, putting a wall behind me and turning so I could see from all angles as I searched my bag blindly for the stun gun.

Once I had it in hand and turned on, I yanked my phone from my back pocket. "Hey, Susan," I said loudly.

The automated AI responded immediately. I didn't want to take my eyes off my surroundings for a second to look at my phone. "Call the Black Claw Police Department."

"Calling now," she responded, and the sounds of a phone ringing came through the earpiece on speaker. Bless technology.

"Black Claw PD, Axel Kingston speaking."

"Axel!" I yelled. "This is Kara Hannon. I'm Rico Kingston's—"

He cut me off. "I know who you are, Kara." His voice was calm and soothing. "What's wrong?"

My voice wavered and I fought to keep it steady enough to get the words out. "I just got home. Someone has been in my house. The front door is standing wide open."

I heard shuffling noises from his end. "Stay calm. Are you inside?"

My eyes kept raking from left to right, trying to make sure nothing changed. No movements, no sounds, nothing. "Yes, I came in the back door. I have my stun gun on and I'm in a corner."

I was close enough to one. If I shifted all the way into the corner, I wouldn't have been able to see my bedroom door. This way I could see if anyone came out of it. I didn't want to close or lock the back door in case Tye was still in the house. I didn't want to go running back out the back door in case he was out there waiting for me. This felt like the safest place.

"Kara, I've already texted my family. They're all on the way. I'm not sure who is closest but stay on the phone with me."

"Okay," I said shakily. My adrenaline was through the damn roof.

"Good. Tell me if anything changes. I'm going to beep in from my cell phone, okay?"

As soon as he said that, the line beeped. I glanced at it long enough to see the strange number and press the button to end the current call and answer the new. "Hey," I said shakily.

"I'm on my way to you," he said. "The cavalry is coming, just hang tight."

"So far nothing," I said. My eyes kept darting between my bedroom and the front door, watching, waiting for Tye to come barreling out at me.

Minutes later, Rico came rushing through the door with no warning. By that time, my nerves were shot, and I gasped in shock, startling so hard I almost dropped my phone. "How did you get here so fast?"

He inhaled deeply, gaze sweeping the area and locking onto my bedroom. "There's nobody here." He growled. "But he was."

"Okay. I'm hanging up now, but I'll be there soon." Axel disconnected the line. At least he was on his way.

I hung up and set the phone and the stun gun on the counter. My adrenaline dissipated now that Rico was here. I knew that with him here, nobody could hurt me.

But then, all the same questions plagued me, and my previous anxiety ramped back up. I needed answers from him so bad it hurt. "Why do you care so much?" I asked as Rico pulled me into his arms.

He still seemed pissed about Tye but looked down at me in concern. "How can you ask that? Because you're my mate. I love you."

I couldn't help the words that slipped from my mouth as the tears fell down my cheeks. "If you're just going to leave me anyway, I wish you wouldn't say things like that."

Chapter 20 - Rico

As soon as she asked me about leaving her, everybody in my family showed up, including half the women. Perfect timing. I hadn't realized that we hadn't had this discussion yet. I assumed that by making plans for school and starting my own business, she would come to the conclusion that I wasn't going anywhere.

"We'll talk when everyone is gone," I growled. I tried to impress upon her my sincerity, but she wouldn't look up at me. She was still freaked out about Tye. I understood.

Maverick came over and took Kara's hand while his wife, Ava, busied herself with Kara's groceries. While their timing could've been better, I was grateful that they'd dropped everything to rush over and help her.

Jury had come in with them and used his extraordinary nose to roam through the house, smelling and making notes.

Kara looked at him like he was crazy, but I knew what he was doing. He was a tracker, meaning he smelled things at a deeper level, much like a bloodhound. I wasn't sure, but Jury probably could outsniff the best hunting dog. Judging by his expression as he passed through again, though, there was as little physical evidence of Tye's presence as there had been at the shop.

Maverick kept Kara preoccupied by asking questions about Tye, and if there was anything else that had happened between them that would possibly spur him to get this personal. From what I knew of him, though, it wouldn't have taken much more than looking at him the wrong way, especially after the incident at the bar.

Kara shook her head. She looked wild behind her eyes. Shock, probably. I tried to send her soothing thoughts and emotions, but we weren't bonded.

Bond her. Soon.

I wasn't arguing with Valor on this one. She needed me as much as I needed her. I decided that when my family left and we sat down for that talk, I would bring it up.

Kara sniffed. "I told you guys what happened in high school. You know what happened at the bar. The only other time I've seen him was at the gym when I was with Rico."

I shrugged and looked at Maverick. "I just told him to stay away from her, but this... this is crossing a line into stalking and is a serious violation. This is the kind of behavior that leads to violence."

Maverick nodded as Jury walked back into the living room. He knew that these things usually escalated into kidnappings, violence, often rape and murder. We had to nip it in the bud, and better now than later. I was afraid of what might happen if we sat on this much longer.

Jury sat on the edge of Kara's coffee table. "From the smell of things, he didn't take anything, but

I can't be sure in your bedroom. Your drawers have been rifled through."

My stomach churned thinking about what he might've been looking for in her dresser drawers. As if invading her home wasn't enough, he had to lower himself to shit like that?

Kara jumped up and ran into her bedroom. "Gross!" she yelled.

I followed quickly with Maverick and Jury on my heels, Axel having just walked in the door. He and Ava crowded in behind us, peering over and between us at the mess.

"What?" I looked around to see if Tye had left some gross calling card or something. Bodily fluid was the first thought that came to mind, and I was both infuriated by the idea and anxious for the evidence to pin him legally.

Kara pointed at her lingerie drawer. "Half of it is gone."

My blood boiled even harder. Valor moved impatiently, and I got a sense like he was pacing. He felt useless in this situation, and I couldn't blame him. My anger would only help so much if I didn't have an outlet, and though Tye was a good target, I'd have to find him first.

Have Jury track him.

I would. Jury would find him for me. My chest rumbled with Valor's enthusiasm.

We piled back out into the living room. "Kara, it would be best if you stayed somewhere else tonight," Maverick said.

"You're welcome to stay with us," Ava chimed in. "We've got Maddox's old room."

I shook my head. "No, she can come to stay at the manor." It was the safest place in Black Claw. We could control every aspect of the land around the manor, set up watches, rotations. He wouldn't be able to reach her there.

But Kara set her jaw adamantly, and I knew her mind was already set. "I will *not* be run out of my home by anyone, much less a high school bully. I've got my stun gun. I will not leave." She was being totally stubborn, and I saw her shutting down right in front of my eyes.

"I'll be right here with you," I assured her. "You'll have protection." If she wasn't going anywhere, neither was I.

Maverick promised they'd find him, even if they had to resort to unconventional means, and they all left us. Kara sat down on the couch and tucked her legs up as she hugged a pillow. Though she insisted on staying, her expression as she curled in on herself was defeated.

I sat beside her and put my hand on her knee, rubbing my thumb back and forth comfortingly. "Hey. They'll find him. And in the meantime, I'm not leaving your side."

She turned confused eyes my way. "How did you get here so fast?"

That was a good question. "I was already on my way," I explained. "I went home, and I was digging into my research when Valor freaked out. I couldn't get him to calm down, and he wouldn't explain. He nearly shifted us, he was so agitated. So I packed a quick bag and came straight over here."

Kara stiffened. She blinked, then smiled. "Valor just told me he felt my distress."

"What were you distressed about?" I asked. "Valor didn't tell me why we had to come, he just kept yelling for me to get over here."

She didn't answer my question, averting her gaze to the floor in front of her. "Are you planning to leave Black Claw?"

How did she remember that? "I told you once that I'd always wanted to be a hermit."

Her fingers tightened their grip on her pillow, but her voice remained calm. "Yes, but did you plan to leave once you knew I was your mate?"

I nodded, going for honesty. "Yes, when I first came here, I never intended to stay permanently. My plan was to stay here long enough to prove to my uncles that I deserved my inheritance. Originally, I had no intention of staying. But things changed. I changed. You saw that for yourself."

But her eyes had hardened, and her voice became razor sharp. "So, you used me."

"I don't know why you're so upset. I told you my plan from the get-go."

She shook her head, and I felt her mood shifting again. "Everyone leaves me. Nobody ever wants to keep me forever." Her heart beat so fast, so erratically, I knew she was in some sort of a panic attack. She began to breathe faster and tears streaked down her cheeks. "I was just something to pass the time for you, wasn't I?"

Damn. She was long gone. I didn't have much experience with panic attacks or anxiety or whatever it was called, but I could hear that her nervous system was out of whack. I wished Charlotte was here. Axel's wife. She knew about the human body and what to do to help.

I tried to pull her close, hoping that contact would help. I remembered the effect her touch had had on Valor and me when we got angry.

But Kara shrugged me off and stood, arms crossed defensively over her chest. "Please leave."

"Kara, stop it. Take a deep breath and calm down and you'll see. You're probably freaked out about all this and doubts are plaguing you. I have no intention of leaving you. Until Tye is sorted out, I'm not leaving at all."

"I want you to go." She backed away from me, her voice wavering. "Now."

What was I supposed to do? My words weren't coming out like they needed to. I just needed to convince her that I was staying, that my plans had changed. Was that really so hard?

"Kara, come on." I knew it had to be her old fears of abandonment making her act like this. She knew I loved her. I'd said the words first. She had to know how much she meant to me. To Valor and me both.

Maybe she was so worried about being abandoned that she wanted to do the abandoning first. Valor rebelled at the idea.

Her breathing got harder and faster and she doubled over. I took a step toward her, but she flung her hands up, warding me off.

"Please," she said pitifully. "Just go."

If I didn't do as she asked, she was going to pass out or something. "Okay, I will. If you promise you'll go lie down and calm down, I'll leave."

She nodded, her eyes bright and watery. "Okay. I will."

"I'm not leaving for good," I promised her. "I'm coming back. In a couple of hours. And I'll have my cousins patrol this street. I can probably get one of them to stay outside and keep watch."

She kept backing toward her bedroom. "Okay. If you go. Promise me that you'll leave. Don't stay outside or something."

Damn it. That's exactly what I'd planned to do. "Damn it, Kara, snap out of this."

"Rico!" she screamed. "I was fine before I met you. I'll be fine after. I know you planned to leave me. You didn't keep it a good enough secret. Now get out!" By the time she finished, her voice had risen into a raw scream. She scrubbed at her face angrily.

I backed as far away as I could and shook my head weakly. I kept my voice soft as I tried once more to explain. "After I realized how much I loved you, the only time I planned to leave Black Claw was to tie up loose ends in Arizona. I was going to ask you to go with me."

"Go. Do it. It'll give me some time away from you. And *if* you come back, Rico—if you come back, maybe we'll talk then." Her breathing had calmed after she screamed, as if the loud noise had gotten through to her or something. Her heart rate slowly eased down into a normal pattern, though her face was still flushed, as I stood with my hands up and back against the front door.

My heart plummeted into my stomach when I registered the meaning in her words. "You can't mean that. You're breaking up with me?" My throat constricted painfully.

"A break, yes. Go. Get out of here."

How had this day gone like this? We'd been so happy just a few hours before.

Valor howled inside me, his heart shattering. I wanted to fall apart, too, but I couldn't. This wasn't the end. I would find a way to fix this.

"Fine," I said in a hard voice. "But when I get back, I'm claiming you. You better be ready for it."

Actions spoke louder than words. I'd give her time to calm down and come out of whatever kind of anxiety attack this was. Then I'd prove my love to her. I fumbled for the doorknob behind me, watching as Kara retreated to her room and slammed the door, then turned and walked away.

Valor freaked as we left, but I got on the phone with Axel before I pulled out of the driveway. He said he'd come himself and sit in a cruiser outside her front door. If anything happened, he'd hear it, and I would be the first to know.

I wasn't completely honest with why I was willing to leave Kara. I had resources of my own to bring Tye down. And Kara wouldn't be happy about them. They weren't the sort of people I wanted anywhere around her, and I knew the sort of favors I'd have to give them to get what I wanted.

Chapter 21 - Kara

He said he'd be gone a few hours. I had lost my ever-loving shit and made him leave, and he said a few hours. He got his cousin to hang out in my street. I felt secure and safe, even after acting like a complete psychopath and making him leave. I did as I said I would and lay down and tried to calm down. I'd fallen asleep, and when I woke, my eyes hurt but I felt a million times better.

And completely foolish. Why had I done that? Talk about going off the deep end.

But then a day passed, and he didn't come back. And my foolish behavior began to seem less idiotic. I went to my jobs on Wednesday without Rico and let the work occupy my thoughts.

I did take my stun gun. I wasn't a complete fool.

And another day passed without a word. I booked my day out completely, throwing myself into my work instead of focusing on my broken heart.

Cynthia had been right. All it had taken was one solid freak-out on my part and Rico had split. It was an unintentional freak-out, borne of ingrained insecurities and feelings I'd done my best to avoid. I hadn't acted like that on purpose. But now I was glad that I had. It showed me early that he didn't have the staying power needed for a long-term relationship.

And now here I was, alone, with all this knowledge about dragons. Should I tell anyone?

Not yet. I couldn't do that to them. They were good people, even if Rico turned out to be a complete slime-bag.

It occurred to me that if all the Kingstons were dragons then Beth had to know. She was mated to one, after all! I decided as soon as we could get together, I'd give her pure hell about not telling me, but of course forgive her right after. After all, I wasn't calling to tell my sister for the same reasons Beth hadn't told me.

But I'd make her buy me a few drinks first.

The worst part was that Cynthia was right.

I avoided going anywhere I would possibly run into her. I even drove to the next town over to grocery shop when I finally ran out of food nearly a week later. I most certainly didn't go anywhere near that damn diner. Or the gym. When a call came through the app to work at the gym, I denied it.

Fuck them.

I used my new security system to make sure everything was well and even figured out how to connect cameras to the same system, so my house was monitored the same way. I put a camera in every room, even the bathroom. I'd already changed the password so Rico didn't have access to the feeds anymore, so nobody would see me sitting on the toilet but me. But I'd be damned if anyone would hide in my house and surprise me.

I'd convinced myself he'd never be back. Tuesday morning, exactly one week after Rico left, I ran into Jury at the gas station. I waited in my car until the lot was empty, then jumped out, cursing myself for not filling up when I'd gone to the grocery store the day before. I could've filled up beside that store and avoided stopping in Black Claw altogether. There were too many people here I didn't want to run into. Especially the Kingstons.

Jury surprised me, though. He pulled up and got out of his car before I could hang up the pump and make my escape.

"Hey, Kara. How are you?"

I nodded but couldn't bring myself to look him in the eye. "Fine, thanks. Hope you're well."

Jury hesitated but put his hand on my arm. "He's coming back."

Nodding, I turned away and blinked back tears as I cut off the pump. The truck wasn't full, but I didn't care. I needed to get away before I made a fool of myself again. "Sure, of course."

"Kara, he's looking for Tye."

I scoffed and shot Jury a look of disbelief. "Okay. Does that mean he can't call?"

Jury opened his mouth to reply, but then he stiffened and grabbed my arm, yanking me close. "Don't move," he whispered.

"What are you doing?" I hissed. I tried jerking my arm away to no avail.

"Did Rico tell you that I'm a tracker?" He put his arm around me and tucked me under his shoulder. It wasn't a sexual or inappropriate move, but I felt protected the same way I had around Rico.

"Of course."

"I've been tracking Tye. He's close. I pulled in when I spotted you and now I can smell him."

My eyes widened, and the edge of panic tingled on my senses. I couldn't look around much under Jury's arm, but I didn't have to wait long. Within seconds, Tye walked around the gas station. His face split into a big grin, but there was nothing happy about it. It was a cruel, sadistic expression, and it only got wider as he walked toward us.

Jury stepped forward and put me behind him. "Don't get any closer."

Tye completely ignored him. "Shut up." He kept walking toward us.

Jury turned his head to speak quietly to me. "Get in the truck and drive directly to the manor. Do you hear me? Straight there."

He was right. Rico might've been gone, but the look on Tye's face was absolutely terrifying. Something was off about him.

"I have to pay for my gas," I whispered.

"Don't worry about that," he replied. "I'll take care of it."

I jumped into the truck and shut the door as Jury kept himself between my truck and Tye. I knew Jury could handle himself better than pretty much any human. Rico had told me the dragons gave them enhanced abilities in their human forms.

My knuckles were white as I gripped the wheel hard, thinking about the look on Tye's face. Going as fast as I could, I turned onto Main and headed out of town. The road up to the Kingston manor house was down Main street on the far end. I'd only been up this way once or twice, but it was the only road in that part of town that headed up into the mountains. Now I knew it was because all that land belonged to the Kingstons, and a lack of roads from town meant they could control if humans came onto their land.

Once I was on the gravel road headed up the mountain, I went faster, bouncing around in my truck. I came around a bend and a strange SUV was pulled off on the side of the gravel road in a small patch of grass. I blew past it, not even slowing down.

My heart raced as I realized the vehicle hadn't been empty as I thought. It pulled out behind me, slinging gravel as it got right on my bumper.

It was reckless to go any faster on this winding, mountainous, gravel road, but I pushed the truck anyway. It was a couple of miles to the manor. I knew Maverick's house was along the way somewhere, but I had no idea where the turnoff was.

As I turned a particularly sharp curve, the SUV hit my back bumper. My truck careened, then slammed onto its side. It all happened so fast. The seatbelt bit into me as my body tried to fall to the ground. I moaned, trying to figure out if I'd hit my head on the steering wheel.

It was over in a flash. One minute I was going around a curve and the next I was hanging from the seatbelt. Damn it. I wasn't confused, though, so that was a good sign. I hadn't hurt my noggin, but I had to get upright.

I twisted my legs out from under the dash and instead of popping the seatbelt free, I slid out of it. If I'd let it go, I would've just collapsed in a clump on the passenger window.

"Freeze." The deep voice meant business. Someone stood outside the truck, pointing a gun through the front window. "Climb out the driver's window." He stood just to the side of a bright ray of sunshine, obscuring his features. It wasn't Tye, though. Did Tye have men working for him that would go to these lengths? This was insanity. Like something from a bad action movie.

I nodded and looked forlornly at my purse. The stun gun was in there. If I could grab it, I might have a chance.

"Don't even think about it." He must've seen me contemplating my purse. "Whatever you're itching to grab, leave it there. I guarantee I can pull this trigger before you can reach it."

Fuck. How had this happened? Maybe I was a little fuzzy.

"Climb out!" he yelled. His voice sounded more panicked than before. I scrambled to do as he said, using the steering wheel and still-buckled seatbelt as leverage. The man still stood in front of the truck, but a second set of hands reached in and grabbed me, yanking me up and out faster than I ever could've gotten myself. I cried out as broken glass from the window scraped across my arm.

As soon as I had my feet on the ground, I started fighting. I'd learned a thing or two over the years and stomped the man's instep as hard as I could.

Nothing surrounded me but woods. But damn, I was safer in Kingston woods than anywhere else. I was surprised these men were brave enough to do this on Kingston land.

I ran as hard and fast as I could, uphill, trying to stay somewhat parallel with where I thought the road was. I held my arm close. I could tell it was bleeding, but not how badly; I didn't have time to stop and look.

The men stayed on my heels. If I tripped like the idiot women that were always being chased in horror movies, I wouldn't be able to get up. Fear, panic, and adrenaline kept my legs pumping.

I also knew they had at least one gun, so I didn't run in a straight line. Thankfully, there were lots of trees to provide cover. Their loud footfalls and panting breaths as they chased me helped me be sure they were moving too fast to shoot.

For a few seconds, I lost the sound of them. I tried to move as quietly as possible, sacrificing a bit of speed to keep quiet. My heart soared when I thought I'd lost them, so I sprinted outright again, hopping over branches and between bushes, uphill toward the Kingston house.

Until an arm came out of nowhere as I was mid-hop. My body curled around it with an oomph, taking my breath for a few seconds as I tried to struggle against my attackers.

When I got my breath, I screamed at the top of my lungs, desperately hoping I was close enough to the manor that the dragons' excellent hearing would pick up my distress.

Didn't Rico say he'd felt me before? He'd felt my extreme upset on the day I'd pushed him out of my life. Maybe he'd feel it now, all the way in Arizona or wherever he was, and call someone here in Black Claw to tell them to look for me.

I kicked and swung my arms wildly, aiming for vital parts. As hard as I fought, though, they overpowered me. "Tye isn't paying us enough for this," one of them said as he wrapped a bandana around my face and gagged me. He had a long, deep scratch down one cheek from my fingernails.

Good.

Soon, they had my hands tied too. I fought until my muscles burned and my throat was raw from screaming, even around my gag. If any of the dragons got close enough, they might've heard me. I had to keep fighting until they came.

With one hand on each of my arms, they marched me back through the woods and out by my wrecked truck. I moaned when I saw it. It would be totaled for sure.

After stuffing me on the floorboard of the back seat of their SUV, I kicked out at them again, getting one in the stomach. They grabbed my ankles hard and tied my feet, blindfolded me with another bandana, then the two assholes got in the front and turned the vehicle around.

I bounced around as they hurried down the gravel road, bumping my elbows and head on the floorboard several times before they finally pulled out onto a smooth, paved road. But they turned left.

Away from town.

Fuck.

They didn't drive all that long, however. I was pulled to my feet. I hoped they'd untie them, but someone lifted me into their arms. The sound of crunching gravel underfoot was the only indication of where I was. Somewhere with gravel.

Super helpful.

We went inside. I heard a door slam shut and the light behind the bandana disappeared. Another door opened, and the man's boots clomped down an old wooden staircase. It smelled damp and musty around us.

The guy holding me dropped me onto a sort of soft surface. A sofa, I was pretty sure. I struggled to sit up with my hands bound behind me and feet still tied together. Silence settled over the room, and my muscles shook. I knew what kind of stuff happened to girls who got kidnapped. I'd seen enough horror movies. If the Kingstons didn't hear me, if they didn't get to me in time, I would die down here.

Sometime later, a door slammed, and another set of boots stomped down the steps. I caught a whiff of smoke and people moving around. Then the bandana around my eyes was ripped off, and I blinked up, squinting to see where I was. It was a large basement that had been converted into a cozy living area. With Tye lounging on a couch across from me, smoking a cigar.

And I wasn't on a sofa. I was on a bed with a really shitty mattress. The smell of the place sunk in. Stale cigars and something even less pleasant.

Tye leaned forward and put the cigar in an ashtray on a small table between us. The other two men were nowhere to be found. "Do you know what it feels like to have people look at you like you're trash? For someone to call your parents and tell them you're a sexual deviant? They told my parents I tried to rape you."

I shook my head, still gagged. I didn't know much about his life after high school. I'd heard rumors that his parents had kicked him out, but I didn't know why.

"After what I was falsely accused of in college, this time they believed it." He snarled his lips at me. "They took care of it last time. Used their money to cover it all up. But this time, you and your boyfriend fucked it all up. You're going to pay for that."

I shook my head. I hadn't told them anything. "No!" I tried to talk around the gag, but Tye stood, towering over me.

I didn't have time to do more than flinch before the back of his hand connected with my cheek. "Someone sent them proof of the college stuff, proof of what happened between us. Videos and pictures. How did you get all that?"

I kept shaking my head as tears streamed down on my face. I cowered, scooting as far back on the bed as I could. Was that what Rico had been doing? Finding information about Tye? Why hadn't he checked in with me or told me what was going on?

"You and your precious boyfriend want to sneak around and make these claims, ruin my life? Well, I'm going to give you something real to complain about, you uppity bitch."

Chapter 22 - Rico

I turned my cell back on as the plane touched down. I'd turned it off the moment I stepped outside of Black Claw, using only the burner phone. It had nearly killed both me and Valor not to contact Kara, but it had to be done. We couldn't risk putting her in danger.

The people I'd gone to were not the sort that I could tell about Kara. If they knew about her, they'd use her against me. I'd gotten all the proof I'd needed of his attack on her on my own. The entire investigation had been done with no mention of my mate's name. All the information I'd suspected I'd find was there. Tye had pulled this shit on several women in the past. Some he'd threatened or bought off himself, some his parents had to step in and handle. This way he could be brought down without Kara being dragged into it legally.

And I'd had to do them a favor in return.

These weren't the same people I'd gone with the last time. We weren't on a joyride around Texas, wooing women, and using our charms to get by. We weren't getting rich older women to pay our way in exchange for the best sex of their lives.

These were human men. Terrible men. And they knew I had a certain skill set. They didn't know it came from being a dragon, but they knew I could get into places and find things others couldn't.

And in exchange for their help tracking down all the proof that Tye was a sick, twisted bastard, they'd required my special skill set to get them into a certain vault.

It just so happened to be in the basement of a casino in Vegas.

It had been the hardest heist I'd ever participated in. But I was sure I'd gotten the job done without the authorities knowing my involvement. And I'd left a very faint clue for them. If the investigators were any good, it would lead them back to my friends, who would spend a very long time in prison. And I'd get off scot-free.

As the seatbelt sign flashed off, my phone began to beep and didn't stop for several seconds. I opened my texting app to see every member of the Black Claw clan had tried to get a hold of me.

And all in the past hour or so.

They all said some variation of requests for me to call them. I dialed Jury first, suddenly terrified it had something to do with Kara. "What's going on?" I nearly yelled. Several passengers near me in the first-class gave me sideways looks.

"Hang on!" he yelled. The sound of wind came through the phone, then abruptly cut off. "I pulled over, but I'm tracking her. Rico, don't freak out." Jury's voice sounded far too calm and controlled. "But Tye has her. He got some help and caught us off guard."

"Tell me what happened. I'm still idling on the runway, waiting to deplane."

"I was tracking him. He got close to her, so I had her get in her truck and go straight to the manor while I stayed with eyes on Tye."

That's what I would've done myself. Kara couldn't have known it, but I didn't leave her unprotected. One of my cousins had been outside her house each night to make sure Tye didn't get to her.

"He must've known we were watching her place. We found her truck turned on its side right in our own fucking driveway. I didn't recognize the scents of the men that got her. I'm driving up the highway now, I just pulled over to talk to you."

"How did Tye get away from you?" I asked in a low voice.

"When Axel found her truck, he called me. I went hunting for her. Tye was with me, so I knew he didn't get her. But now that I'm on her trail, his scent is mixing in. I think two men got her, took her this way, and Tye followed."

"Where?"

"Toward some of the rental cabins not far from our property. They're fairly secluded. Tye probably thought they'd be a good place to hide her."

The instant people began standing, I leaped into the aisle and shoved toward the front. Thank goodness I was already in first class. "Sorry, I've got an emergency at home," I said loudly. "Please let me off the plane!"

I left my bag in the overhead compartment. I could come to get it later.

People moved out of the way. "Jury, get back on the road. Send me coordinates as soon as you have them."

I hung up and jogged as fast as I could through the tiny airport. I didn't want to raise anyone's suspicions, but I had to get to my truck. I'd parked it in the long-term parking lot at the airport, thankfully. I could've had someone pick it up, but I wasn't sure when I was returning. I didn't want anyone to have to drop anything and come collect me.

The coordinates came through just as I unlocked the truck. I mapped it. Not too far away. Maybe a half-hour. If I could've shifted, I would've gotten there in minutes, but there was too much risk of being spotted. I had to drive. I punched the steering wheel and pressed the pedal to the floor.

My mind buzzed with worry as I headed toward the spot my phone directed me to. The drive felt like the longest of my life.

When my phone rang, I looked at it, but it showed no call on the screen. It took me a second to realize it was the burner phone.

"What?" I barked.

"This is confirmation that the package was delivered successfully. My man just got back."

Oh, shit. He fucked up. He fucked up bad. "Wait a minute. Your man wasn't supposed to deliver the package until now. He should still be in the target's town."

Silence.

"You fucked up, didn't you?" I asked. I didn't give him time to respond. "I knew I should've gone to someone else. I did you a much bigger favor than you did me. And you fucking screwed it up. This concludes our business. Don't expect to hear from me again."

I threw the burner phone as hard as I could and listened to it shatter on the pavement as I drove about twenty miles per hour over the speed limit. I was skating at the edge of panic, my mind playing out multiple scenarios that could've happened in the time Tye and his associates had taken her.

Jury stood on the side of the road close to the coordinates he gave me. I slammed on the brakes and pulled over. He motioned for me to get out. "We should go on foot from here."

Valor was ready to kill. He would've shifted and flown directly to Kara. From here, I could faintly smell her, and it drove him mad. I gritted my teeth as he thrashed and tried to force the change.

Jury eyed me carefully. "Come on, I've got a lock on her. We can't shift here. Can you control Valor?"

Slowly, Valor eased back, and I shook the pressure out of my head, willing him to understand.

I will allow you to handle it for now. But if it doesn't go well, I will *take over to protect our mate.*

"He'll behave as long as we're doing well," I said.

"Fair enough." Jury turned and walked into the woods. I followed hot on his feet.

I would've walked a thousand miles to save Kara, but we made it in about twenty minutes.

"Two guards," Jury whispered. "I recognize their scents from our driveway. They're the two that took her. I still only smell them, Tye, and Kara."

I nodded. "Let's take care of them."

We walked out of the woods as close as we could get to the luxury cabin. They stood in front of the door but weren't doing a great job guarding. We were nearly on top of them before they noticed us.

Hand-to-hand combat was a joke with these two humans. We knocked their guns away and within seconds they were both unconscious.

"I already called my dad," Jury whispered. "So keep in mind, the Black Claw PD are on their way."

I nodded and opened the door, going inside silently. The living room and kitchen were empty. Kara's scent was here, but she must've been in another room. I was heading around to what looked like a bedroom when a sound stopped me in my tracks.

All logic left me when I heard her scream. She was at a lower level. I sprinted back to the kitchen, nearly ripping the door to the basement from its hinges. I launched myself down the stairs, skipping several as I flew down them and into the large underground room.

Tye was on top of Kara, trying to force her knees open as she screamed around a gag. Her hands were bound, and frayed ropes lay on the bed at her feet. Amazing how much detail I noticed as I all but flew across the room. Her ankles and wrists were red and raw, and there was a gash on one arm, but she hadn't noticed me as she fought and struggled against Tye.

And her clothes, though a bit ripped, were still on. Thank the heavens.

I put a hand on Tye's shoulder and yanked him across the room with one hard pull.

Kara spotted me and sank back on the bed in relief, tears pooling in her eyes.

At some point after leaving town, I'd lost the ability to feel her emotions. It was like cutting off the lifeline I'd made with her. As soon as I saw her again, I felt it. A faint impression of her emotions. She was scared and in a panic, but largely unhurt.

I might've been able to control myself, but as I looked at Kara, Tye punched me in the kidney.

It didn't hurt that much. Just enough to send me into a full blood rage. I roared in fury and turned on him, losing myself in a red haze. The noises and voices around me were muffled, the pain in my knuckles only a faint idea. The next thing I knew, Kara had her arms wrapped around me. "Stop! You're going to kill him!"

I looked down to see Tye covered in blood. He was still underneath me, and my knuckles were stained bright red with his blood and mine. They healed even as I watched them. I'd busted them open on his face.

He wasn't dead. I heard his heart beating. But I'd rearranged his face. He'd never look pretty enough to try to seduce a woman ever again. My lip curled at the fact that I hadn't done more, but I was also glad Kara had stopped me when she did.

Jury must've gotten Kara loose while I went berserker. I nodded my thanks at him just as the smell of my family hit me. I registered footsteps overhead. The police were here. Jumping up, I wiped Tye's blood on a blanket on the floor by the bed, then pulled Kara into my arms and held on tight. She clung to me. "I'm so sorry," I whispered. "I shouldn't have left. I thought I was helping, but I should've stayed and never left your side."

We hugged each other for a while. Maverick and James got Tye upstairs and into an ambulance as I kept reassuring Kara that I'd never leave her again. "I want to claim you, to make you mine, as soon as you will let me. I'll do it right now if you'll let me." I knew Valor was giving her similar reassurances.

I wouldn't let her go, not to give statements to the police. They were my family, and they understood the whole mate thing, so they let it slide.

"How'd you know where she was?" Maverick asked as if he didn't already know.

"I was following," Jury said. "We had a bad feeling. I called the police when they took her, and I figured out where they were. Rico was close by and I knew we couldn't wait."

"Sounds reasonable," Maverick said. Of course, Mav knew exactly how we found her, but he had to put something down for the record.

It was a good thing Mav had jurisdiction up here in the county. Otherwise, we'd have had to come up with a more detailed explanation.

"Make sure you don't leave town," Maverick said with a wink at Kara.

She stayed quiet, still reeling from the ordeal.

"No problem." I buried my face in Kara's hair, taking in the cinnamon scent of her that I'd missed so much. "I'm never leaving again." My heart ached for what she'd been through, thinking I was never coming back. I hated that I hadn't given her more information or sent word that I was coming back. I vowed then and there to make it up to her for the rest of her long, extended life. Starting by biting her and making her harder to hurt.

As soon as they gave us permission, I took Kara home. Jury caught a ride back with Mav after bringing me my truck. When we got to her place, I jogged around the truck and picked her up, carrying her straight to the bathroom. The relief of having her in my arms was intense. I squeezed her tight.

She squeaked. "I'm happy to be back with you, too, Rico," she said with a laugh. "But I can't breathe."

After relaxing my hold and setting her down in the bathroom, I ran a shower and we both stood under the spray, still hugging each other close. Eventually, I let her go long enough to gently wash every inch of her body. "Wash it all away," I said. "Let the water take the grossness of that place with it."

She held her head back and breathed deep, her breasts rising and falling as her emotions flowed through the bond. She still felt shocked and upset, but it quieted, and a sense of calm came over her.

I quickly washed myself, getting all the blood off my hands and arms, then dried my mate and carried her to bed.

Wrapping myself around her, I snuggled close, both of us completely naked. "I'm so sorry," I whispered. "I thought I was helping."

"Why did you leave?" She looked up at me with sorrowful eyes. "I didn't mean it. I think I was having a panic attack. I didn't want you to leave."

"I went to visit some old friends," I explained. "I took the opportunity to find some old cohorts and use their abilities to get info on Tye. They took it to his parents, but they did it too soon. They were supposed to do it after I got back in town so that if it enraged him, I could protect you. But they took it too soon. That's why he was angry enough to have you grabbed."

Tears rolled down her cheeks. I realized now that she was clean that a bruise was blossoming on one of them. I rubbed the pad of my thumb over the slight discoloration. "I should've killed him."

"No," she exclaimed. "You'd be in jail."

"If Jury hadn't called the cops already, I could've covered it up," I insisted. "Before I went to my associates for their help, I went to Arizona. I told my grandfather I didn't want my inheritance. It's not important to me anymore. I asked for enough money to take some college classes and help bankroll a PI and security firm here in Black Claw."

She stared at me with wonder on her face and another tear escaped. I wiped it away gently. "What did he say?"

This was the best part. "They were so happy for me that they gave me the full inheritance. They said I'd become the man they'd known I could be all along." I sighed and told her the rest of it. "I told them the truth about where I went and why. And what I did. They said that considering I set everything up so that the true criminal would take the fall, they could forgive the slip into my old way of life."

I pursed my lips before telling me the rest. "They also said if I ever did anything like that without consulting them first, I'd find myself out on my ass. I believe Uncle Perry used the expression, 'up shit creek,'" I said ruefully.

I had no plans of delving back into that life. I knew I'd changed because not a single part of me had enjoyed the heist.

Kara laughed and pressed a soft kiss to my lips. "I'll help them." Her face went serious before she kissed me again. "Claim me," she whispered. "If you mean it, and you're never leaving me again, claim me."

Valor let out a cross between a growl and a howl, and instantly, my dick hardened. "You're not up for sex," I said.

"Does it have to be sex?" she asked.

It does not.

I laughed. "No. No, it doesn't." I'd be aching, but that was okay. If it made her feel more secure to have it done that way, I was happy to do it. More than happy. I was ecstatic.

She turned her head and exposed her neck. I had no idea what to do.

Let me.

I relaxed and let Valor take the lead. He used me and settled his teeth on her neck gently. He was silent in my head, so I knew he was explaining things to her.

"Do it," she whispered.

Even though she was pretty insistent, Valor took the time to get her more in the mood. He used me to kiss her neck, nuzzling and caressing until she pushed back against me with a feeling of urgency coming through the bond. When her senses were loosened and she'd relaxed her body against mine, he bit down, and the world exploded in my mind. My tentative connection with Kara turned vibrant and bright. I knew that she was happy. She felt safe and relieved.

And horny. The bite had caused her core to drench; I could smell it. Without disturbing my teeth, still gripping her neck, she shifted herself so I could slip inside her.

I moaned as she cried out in pleasure when I filled her. Biting harder, I watched the connection in my mind pulse with bright, happy colors. This was the rightest thing in the world. The best decision I'd ever made.

She was mine, and I was hers. And I spent the rest of the night proving it to her, as many times as I could.

Chapter 23 - Kara

I'd had a lot of trauma in my life, from my junkie parents to my foster home and then jumping to my first failed relationship. I'd been beaten, left alone, and scarred in a variety of ways. I'd been assaulted, kidnapped, and nearly raped. But I was happier now than I had ever thought possible for someone like me. I was broken, but then Rico came along and gave me the courage to pick myself up and patch myself back together, and he would say the same about me. We made each other better people.

We were fated.

When the trial was over, we didn't celebrate. Tye and his friends were going to jail for a very, very long time, and that was enough. Attempted murder, attempted rape, kidnapping, and a slew of other charges thanks to the information Rico's acquaintances had dug up. His parents paid out an *insane* amount of money for my 'pain and suffering' as a part of the settlement, and I'd filed a civil suit on top of the criminal one.

No way I'd touch that money. I donated every penny to a local domestic violence shelter, and I really hoped it made a difference in someone else's life. We had Rico's trust fund if we ever needed it, anyway. I did consider, however, looking for my new apprentice there. Maybe I could give another woman the same opportunity I was given to grow and put herself back together.

Independence could go a long way in bolstering one's confidence, and maybe that was all they needed to get started.

Rico hadn't left my side since the kidnapping. We'd done everything together pretty much all the time. Our time being joined at the hip was coming to a close, though, because he had two classes on some computer... something or other coming up this week. I was so proud of him for following through with his new dreams and couldn't wait to see what he did with them.

When my dad found out what happened, he insisted I start coming over for more self-defense lessons. Rico was all for it, and I loved the time it gave me with the old man. Plus, after what I went through, I wanted all the self-defense training I could get. When you're put in a situation where you have to fight for your life, there is never too much training.

Rico was at the kitchen table when I walked in, his head buried in his laptop. He'd spent a lot of time like that since deciding to go into the security business. Even though he was going to take some classes, he said he'd learned so much watching videos online, he wasn't sure classes would be necessary.

I'd encouraged him to take them anyway.

He paused his video as I walked by. I popped a kiss on top of his head and opened the fridge. "Need anything? A bottle of water?"

As soon as I turned back toward the table from the fridge, I realized something was weird. He was gone. On his laptop was a note.

Bedroom.

I walked into the bedroom to find rose petals and candles everywhere. Rico sat on one knee in the middle of the room. In his hand was a black velvet ring box. "I saved every penny that I made doing real work and used it to buy this," he said. His face was full of hope and happiness. And through the bond, love poured toward me like gasoline fueling a flame. My head felt light as I stepped into the room.

He didn't have to say the words.

"Yes!" I exclaimed. "I'll marry you. I'll marry you right now!"

He surged forward and took me into his arms, and finally, for the first time in my life, I felt whole.

Chapter 24 - Kara

It was the biggest wedding Black Claw had ever seen. We'd transformed the front yard of the Kingston manor and invited half the town.

Once Rico had asked me to marry him, the other couples had gotten some sort of bug about it, and the next thing I knew, we were all engaged.

I'd always thought I'd have a big wedding, always dreamed about it. I never thought it would be like this.

And there had been quite a few bumps along the way. With four couples getting married, the brides had several arguments. But somehow, it always worked out. We figured it out.

Harley was irrationally fanatic about the flowers. They had to be perfect. I would've thought she'd be all about the hair, but she didn't care so much about that. That was Abby. She'd insisted we all have completely different hairstyles and veils.

That had worked itself out just fine, too, as we all wanted different things.

Our dresses were totally different as well. The guys' tuxes, though, we'd agreed they should match.

Picking colors had been another nightmare. We finally narrowed it down to three that we all were happy with, then drew straws.

Teal and lighter teal had won. It was my first pick, so I tried to hide my gloat.

The last argument had been about how to do the service. Four different services were a long time for everyone to sit in the uncomfortable chairs in the grass. Especially as we'd chosen to get married in the summer.

In the end, we did one service, with each of us writing our own vows. The order went by age of couple.

Stefan and Harley went first, with Harley in a short dress with a flared skirt. Next, Jury and Abby. Abby wore a Cinderella gown with long, lace sleeves and a flowing train. It wasn't a dress I would've chosen in a million years, but on her it was perfection.

I dabbed at my eyes as my best friend married her mate. Maddox and Bethany made a gorgeous couple, and Bethany looked perfect in her close-fitting dress with a mermaid skirt. She had a long veil and the dress was covered in beads.

And then it was my turn. After glancing down to make sure my dress—a filmy, body -hugging dress with a slit all the way up to my thigh—looked right before all the gazes in the yard were on me, I made Rico say his vows first.

He looked at me with tears in his eyes as he spoke. "Kara." He stopped and cleared his throat, but I knew he was holding back tears. We'd been together over a year now, and I'd never been closer to anyone in my life. I turned the gigantic diamond engagement ring around on my finger under my bouquet as I waited for him to get it together, smiling encouragingly. "I never thought this would happen. Hell, I never thought I'd be in a place where I'd live amongst family, much less have a m—" He cut off and cleared his throat again. He'd almost said mate in front of the big crowd of humans. "Fiancée and soon-to-be wife. I'm so very thankful that you came into my life. My boss." He chuckled and looked down at the notes in his hand. "I forgot I had these." The crowd tittered with laughter, but he still didn't bother reading them.

His gaze returned to me. "Thank you for not giving up on me. Thank you for being so excited when I shared all my secrets with you." He winked at me, reminding me of how giddy I'd been to find out he was a dragon shifter. "Thank you for being you, and lastly, thank you for being mine." He growled out the last word, and the crowd chuckled once again. A little reminder that Valor was a part of this, too.

The tears were absolutely pouring down my cheeks by then. Rico pulled a hankie out of his inner pocket and handed it to me. I dabbed and turned toward the Rico's grandfather, who was acting as our officiant, to delicately blow my nose. The crowd chuckled again, but I wasn't embarrassed. I knew most of them and they wouldn't have laughed out of cruelty. Besides, when I turned back, I noticed quite a few of them dabbing their own eyes.

My turn. I didn't have notes either. I'd memorized my vows word for word; I was pretty sure they'd be engraved in my mind forever. "Rico Kingston. Boy, I never thought I'd be marrying a Kingston." I turned to the crowd for my only joke. "Sorry, ladies. I got the last one."

Rico's Uncle Perry stood halfway out of his seat and raised his hand. "Uh, I'm still available. This town seems to breed gorgeous women, so yeah. I'm available."

The crowd really laughed then, and Rico's cousins from Arizona all clapped him on the back. I laughed with them and waited for the crowd to go silent again before continuing. "We've both had crazy, not always great, lives. We both know what it is to be lonely, to be left behind." He smiled sadly at my words. "But we don't have to feel that way anymore. We're going to be together for a very long time, and I think we both mean forever when we say these vows." Rico took my hands under the bouquet, wrapping his fingers around my closed ones. "I promise to give you a chance to explain when you say things all wrong. And I promise to try not to get pissed all the time...only when you really deserve it."

Okay, maybe I had one more joke in there. "And I love you, Rico." I leaned in and pressed my cheek to his with my face away from the crowd. "And I love you, too, Valor," I whispered. The humans wouldn't be able to hear me, but all the dragons suddenly got something in their eyes. I glanced at the crowd in time to see them all shift and wipe at their faces.

I love you too, my mate. Even if you do need this odd human ritual.

I stifled a giggle.

"By the power vested in me as the leader of the Maverick clan," Gramps said. The humans would just have to wonder why the Mavericks called themselves a clan. Maybe we could say they were Scottish. "And by the World Wide Web and State of Colorado, I now pronounce all of you, separately, husband and wife!" He chuckled as we watched his face, waiting for the big moment. The photographers were strategically placed to get the kisses without capturing each other as well.

"You may kiss your brides!" He threw up his hands and as Rico bent me backwards in a dizzying dip and pressed his lips to mine, flashbulbs went off like crazy and the guests hooted and hollered.

And then we were one. In mind, body, soul, and now, by law.

Printed in Great Britain
by Amazon

79164523R00149